4 December, 2010

To Anna,

Charity
Begins at Home

a little light reading for dark December days!

BETHANY GOLDPAUGH BROWN

love,
Bethany

iUniverse, Inc.
New York   Bloomington

Charity Begins at Home

Copyright © 2010 Bethany Goldpaugh Brown

All rights reserved. No part of this book may be used or reproduced by any means, graphic, electronic, or mechanical, including photocopying, recording, taping or by any information storage retrieval system without the written permission of the publisher except in the case of brief quotations embodied in critical articles and reviews.

This is a work of fiction. All of the characters, names, incidents, organizations, and dialogue in this novel are either the products of the author's imagination or are used fictitiously.

iUniverse books may be ordered through booksellers or by contacting:

iUniverse
1663 Liberty Drive
Bloomington, IN 47403
www.iuniverse.com
1-800-Authors (1-800-288-4677)

Because of the dynamic nature of the Internet, any Web addresses or links contained in this book may have changed since publication and may no longer be valid. The views expressed in this work are solely those of the author and do not necessarily reflect the views of the publisher, and the publisher hereby disclaims any responsibility for them.

ISBN: 978-1-4502-2803-9 (pbk)
ISBN: 978-1-4502-2844-2 (ebook)

Printed in the United States of America

iUniverse rev. date: 8/2/10

To Ione, Mother and Matt, and in
memory of my father and Maggie

April 17, 1997

"Dear Mother," Charity wrote. She always called her mother "Mother", not Mom, or anything else. Call things by their right names, that's the beginning of wisdom, at least if you're an ancient Chinese sage, she thought. Hmph, if that's the case, I should write "Dear Matriarch." Nevertheless:

Dear Mother,

Thank-you for your last letter and the news clippings. I'm sorry I haven't written sooner. I'm just not keeping up with correspondence like I used to. (Besides, I hardly have anything to say to you and I'm mad at you for your criticism in that last letter. Thank-you, indeed!) I'm sorry that you feel I'm being "taken advantage of" and that I ought to "put my foot down" and insist that Felipe get a job. He's had them before and he'll have them again. But (never begin sentences with a conjunction; Charity heard her mother's voice) BUT, Charity wrote firmly, I feel it's my moral obligation to take care of those at home. "Charity begins at home" you always told me, and you DID name me Charity (she heaped coals on her mother's head with that one, as she had never liked her name until recently, when she actually begin to apply it.)

The phone rang. Charity put her pen down. Normally, she let the answering machine pick up her calls (she loathed talking on the phone) but she really didn't want to be writing this letter to her mother. It was Marney, her quasi-friend. Actually, she wasn't much of a friend at all. She was more of an acquaintance/colleague. "Can you cover for me tomorrow at work? I have out-of-town guests." Hmmm—it meant extra money; also it would be helping Marney. Just how far should she carry this charity business, anyway? "All right, sure." (Why not? She had nothing planned for the week-end, and the extra money was always welcome.) "What time? "Your first appointment is at 11:00." Okay, bye. Back to the letter to Dear Matriarch.

Well, mother I hope you're feeling better. I'm a little worried about this recurring illness. (It's probably your parsimonious husband. He might be rich, but he's so stingy! And he wants you to be, too! "Never begin a sentence with..." AND he always makes me feel unwelcome. How am I supposed to visit you? I live 600 miles away.)

Let me know when you want to come visit next. Anytime is okay. I'll take the time off from work–I'd like to do that. Hope to hear from you soon.

Love,
Charity

> Now to send this off. Maybe I should have Andrew write a line or two to his grandma? Next time.

April 20

After mailing her letter, Charity mused on her name. As a child, she had hated it. She remembered sitting in the kitchen at 4, having just returned from nursery school. "Why did you name me Charity?" she had demanded, as only a 4 year old can demand. "Why didn't you name me something else, like Sally?" Charity couldn't remember what her mother said at that time, but it must have come up again, when she was older, because she remembered her mother's crisp reply, "I liked the name Charity. I thought it was cute." Cute!

Another time, around early adolescence, when Charity had remarked she didn't like her second cousin's name–Rachel–her mother replied that it had almost been Charity's name. Later, Charity realized she liked that name much better, and wished her mother had followed through and called her Rachel instead. She felt Rachel suited her. She felt she had an inner self who WAS a Rachel. As a matter of fact, she had three inner selves: Charity 1, Charity 2 and Rachel. This must have been sometime around college.

It wasn't until later, much later, that Charity began to muse about her name, what it meant literally, and what it meant to her personally. At about 40, she realized, along with a newly awakened sense of social and moral responsibility, how suitable a name it was for her.

She was charitable; she liked to give. She wasn't rich, far from it, she was always struggling to pay her bills, but she honestly felt that you needed to give whatever you could back to the world, to your fellow humans, and if you weren't able to give on a grand, global scale, you had to begin where you could: at home.

April 21

Monday brought school for Andrew, and for Charity. She taught English in a private school for delinquent boys, adolescent boys. It was, in many ways, a charitable act, a donation of time and energy. Salaries at The Academy were low, responsibilities and hours high. But she loved it, she kept telling herself. She loved the boys, and felt she was doing valuable, important work.

Monday was vocabulary day. The eighth grade was reading "A Tale of Two Cities" and today's words had to do with Charles Darnay's first trial. The boys knew all about court terminology. They had all been in court at least several times.

"What's acquitted?" Allen asked.

"You know, it's when the judge lets you off!" yelled Mike.

"Look it up in the dictionary" Charity said, for the nth time that day.

"Why we always be lookin these words up in the dictionary, not on the computer?" Danny grumbled.

Charity thought about the speech of some of her students. It really wasn't street English. It was straight out of the 17th century, or earlier. It was pure Shakespeare. It was no accident that her students actually understood Shakespearian language better than their public school peers. It was closer to their vernacular.

April 22

It was Tuesday; only Tuesday. Earth Day, as a matter of fact. Charity wanted a Tee shirt printed with "I survived The Academy Earth Day."

The Academy , she silently snorted. What a joke. You take illiterate, and passionately devoted to staying illiterate, court-placed adolescent boys, put them in a residential school (didn't they used to be called reform schools?) and then try to "upgrade the standards" by calling it "The Academy" like it was some sort of fancy prep school. It was like putting a Band-aid on gangrene.

The day had started with a wildlife show. (Not the students, this time, an imported wildlife lecturer.) When he brought out the owl he had hatched from an egg, Charity heard Carlos behind her say, "YO, that nigga's big!" She had to laugh. The kids were definitely uniquely true to their own characters.

Then, they had the task of dividing up into groups to do plantings around the grounds and a clean up of the ever-present litter. Invariably, the kids complained

"What d' we have ta do this work for? Don't we hire janitors and yard cleaners?"

You'd think they actually were in a prep school, the way they carried on like spoiled snobs.

"Yo! I better not git bit by a bee! If I git poison ivy, I'll sue!"

And so on, throughout the afternoon.

April 23

The kids began taking over. They invaded her dreams at night. They began to creep into the entries she made in her journal. They pawed through anything of hers that was not locked up. She began to feel like she was their personal property. Even Andrew didn't command so much of her attention. Of course, Andrew wasn't so needy, and these kids were, which was part of the problem. Where there's a need, there's a nurturer, and Charity was a compulsive nurturer. To a point. When El-leek came late to class, obviously limping, complaining he had to walk slowly, he was in so much pain, she couldn't help herself. She burst out, "Oh, poor Leeky!" He gave her the kind of rolled-eyes look Andrew had perfected, and started laughing, her remark being so unexpected. When he left, later, she noticed he was not limping.

April 24

Although Charity would not admit this to many people, especially her Fundamentalist Christian friends, she sometimes consulted oracles, channelers, tarot readers, Santeros; even the daily astrology column in the newspaper.

Sometimes the results amazed her. Sometimes they just made her laugh, especially when the message was an open-ended one, such as today's: "Resolution of a spiritual or erotic nature." What? Which one? Either? Both? How?

Sometimes, when she read the I Ching, she was amused by the line, "Better not to move in any direction whatsoever." Or, "It will be advantageous to move in any direction."

April 25

On Friday, Charity received an unusually high phone bill. Upon looking it over, she realized it was mostly from calling card calls, made from phone booths. Immediately, she suspected Andrew, who had access to the card number so he could check in with her when he was out. When she mentioned to him that the card use was out of control, he said "I want to look at that phone bill." When he looked, he said "Mom, these aren't calls I made. Think about it- why would I call Newburgh ten times? And who do I know in California? Or Queens?" He was becoming visibly irate. "Somebody is using that card! I'm going to find out who! Someone owes us hundreds of dollars!"

Now that Charity realized someone had used the card without authorization, she began to wonder who. She envisioned a drug dealer with a gun slinking from pay phone to pay phone in the seedy side streets near the high school. She didn't want Andrew going up against that. Then she thought about the Academy kids. Some of them were certainly inclined to steal, use drugs and people's phone cards, or anything else they could get their hands on, and wouldn't think twice about it.

Damn! Charity thought. Why couldn't they steal her car instead? It needed replacing, it was insured, she could file a claim if it was stolen and be reimbursed! The car refused to die, it needed repairs she couldn't afford, but it kept on running. And the kids wouldn't steal it, either.

April 27

Charity's father, a family doctor, had been, by all appearances, a workaholic. Charity wondered, not infrequently, if she inherited his tendencies. She often wondered this on days like today, when she was working for the seventh day in a row, and had the week ahead of her, five more days before the possibility of one day off. No mind, she would enjoy that one day off. She told herself, it wasn't that she wanted to work all those hours out of some obscure obsession, some compulsive drive, no she felt- she knew - that the money earned from teaching didn't meet her family's financial needs, so she had to do something extra to make up the difference and that something was working in a hotel spa health club whenever she could, which was on the weekends. She worked as a massage therapist there and she also had a small after-school practice in her house. Working at the hotel provided certain pluses; the health club receptionist booked all the appointments and took all the flak from arrogant or disgruntled guests. Sophia was admirable in that she did all this graciously and efficiently. One of the drawbacks, besides the nearly hour's drive, was that it was next to impossible to develop a working relationship with clients whom you saw once or maybe twice at most. You didn't get to address or correct their problem areas or their habitual misuse as she had been so thoroughly trained to do. Guests often commented to her or to Sophia about how unusually wonderful her technique was. Charity knew it wasn't just the technique. It was a certain caring, a type of nurturance that could be delivered in a half hour or so that she tried to bring to her clients. However, occasionally she met characters whose personality traits were so strong she would never forget them. There was Delores who was the adopted child of Auschwitz survivors and a seeker of knowledge, of health, of wisdom. And there was Cynthia who was a designer and regularly traveled to Europe.

April 28

"Jesse" remarked Allen "You just stressin' youself out for nothing."

"Miss, I need your help finding this." Jesse was turning red with the effort of his protest about the assignment. "This word's not in this dictionary."

Charity wearily made a mental note to order more dictionaries, the kind with more lucid entries.

"Man, why can't we use the computers for this?"

"I'm not a man" said Charity automatically.

"Guess you're not" muttered Mike. Monday again. Lunch duty. Team meeting. Charity had a cold; her assistant was out. Monday again.

As a reward for slogging through the Three Musketeers, Charity permitted the 7th graders to see the video.

"Yo, that nigga's dumb!" yelled one, when D'Artagnan went after the Man with a Scar. "Stubborn, like your father" said the video.

"That's called ugly there," said Ahmeek, when the jailer appeared "looks like a crack head in my neighborhood."

"Miss, did they have guns back then?" Charity liked when they drew parallels between classic fiction and their lives.

"That Cardinal's an evil dude" "He's a good actor, makes people wanna kill him"

"Miss, do people like the musketeers?"

"Hell, yeah, man, they help people!"

April 29

Charity defined: American Heritage Dictionary

1. Good will or kind feelings toward others.
2. Tolerance and leniency in judging others.
3. a kind or generous act. help or relief to the needy.
4. an institution or fund established to help the needy. (first written down in 1137 in Middle English and spelled Carited from Latin Caritas.)

A student's dictionary of definitions:

1. infinity - 4 ever
2. Engulf - I don't know
3. Scheme - a bad deal
4. stout - fat and lard
5. frantic - full wit anxiety
6. disclose - close something
7. berserk - crasy
8. childhood - _____ (this from a student who basically didn't have one)
9. witness - a person that seen something

"Charity suffereth long and is kind; Charity envieth not; Charity vaunteth not itself, is not puffed up; doth not behave itself unseemly, seeketh not her own, is not easily provoked, thinketh no evil, rejoiceth not in inequity, but rejoiceth in the truth; beareth all things, believeth all things, hopeth all things, endureth all things. Charity never faileth...

And now abideth faith, hope, charity, these three; but the greatest of these is charity." King James version of the Bible.

Charity felt discouraged. What did it all mean? What was it all adding up to? Who was she, anyway? Not enough financial resources to be an institution. Not enough selflessness to be pure feeling of tolerance or kindness. Not enough sense of self to be the greatest of these three.

Charity was worried about Andrew, too. He seemed depressed and completely burned out on school. The trouble was, he was a junior and only had about two months left of school. She encouraged him to do his best to hang on until June. She tried to look into a program where he could take his senior year of high school and first year of college together at the local community college. She hoped he wasn't falling into drug use or other damaging habits. She hoped he believed in God. She hoped he was being looked over by a guardian angel. She hoped he would do well. She hadn't done particularly well herself, her junior year of high school and had been pretty disgusted with school by her senior year, but she had gone on to do much better and to truly enjoy college. She just wanted him to be healthy, whole, and happy. How could she protect him from all the tensions and violence of the world? How could she keep him from the self doubts and self destructive habits that the world inflicted on him from every side.

April 30

It was finally warm weather. Charity opened the windows in her schoolroom. A breeze rattled the Venetian blinds, drawing attention to the open windows and away from A Tale of Two Cities.

"Miss, can you shut the window? Bees will come in and get us!" yelled Ahmeek.

"I'll take care of them if they do" Charity reassured him.

"What could you possibly do to a bee?" Ahmeek snorted.

"I'd snuff it!" Charity retorted.

The whole class sat up in amazement; then snickered. It was so seldom she used their slang that they didn't know she knew it. When it was obvious that she did, it sounded so misplaced that they laughed.

It took a good while to get them back on track when she made a comment like this but Charity decided once in a while that it was worth it.

May 1

May Day. Charity and Grace, another teacher at the Academy, were scheduled to take a group of kids to The Farm, a supposedly joint venture with a supposed "living history museum farm" group 25 minutes from the Academy. The whole project, dreamed up by a group of city people on The Farm's board and the city bred director of the Academy was supposed to introduce the kids to "the joys of nature and the value of animals as therapists." The Board at the Academy, who had as little to do with either the school or animals as possible, thought this was a wonderful idea on paper. They envisioned "tongues in trees, books in brooks, and sermons in stones" as the kids received outdoor lessons and a good education all at the same time. Charity thought, grimly, that the Board at either place, Academy or Farm, hadn't really taken that quote in context. If they had, they would have realized that the quote from As You like It began with "Sweet are the uses of adversity" and adversity was what was most present in the lives of the Academy kids. The kids were determined to maintain the status quo.

May 3

Saturday's mail brought a notice that Andrew was failing math, a bank notice that her account was overdrawn, and an appeal from the Academy's board for "charitable donations". Ha! Charity thought. Working for what they pay isn't donation enough? How had her name gotten on that list anyway? Also, there were several overdue bill notices. It did not bring a check from the hotel health club for the days she had covered for Marny.

Charity had been saving a few dollars for the weekend, in hopes that she could actually do something in her leisure time. Her husband might actually join her, if and when he felt it was appealing to him. The money rapidly went for:

emergency Pepto-Bismol for her husband's recurring stomach problem

Andrew's SAT fee

gas for her car

So much for weekend fun. It always went that way. Either she was called to fill in at the hotel, taking up a day off, or if she managed to have a day free of obligations, she had no money to even pay for gas to get there, much less an admission fee. Charity dreamed of a vacation, a real vacation, of a weekend spent in leisurely pursuits, renewing herself, or even of dinner out in a restaurant.

She feared she was becoming a drudge. Charity wondered just when she might be able to start giving to Charity.

May 4

Charity despaired of ever having a nice, large house, but what for? Her dreams of an intact family long ago given up, her own space, a big enough bathroom, minus the mold. She frustrated herself by taking out design and historical home magazines from the library. She'd then sit and dream of transforming her small, overstuffed ("this was always an overstuffed, quirky house" her landlady said once) dusty and somewhat dim house into one with space, charm, and privacy. A hedge in front. A spiral staircase to the attic. Finish the attic, with a new bathroom, bigger, better. Add to the deck, above and below, make it an enclosed greenhouse below. Put in cedar closets and a housewide dehumidifier system. In that case, better get new electric, upgrade to 220. Put in a new half bath. Better upgrade the septic, while we're at it. Add a sump pump, dormer windows in the attic, a tiny porch off a Palladian window in the back of the new attic room. Sounds like building a new house!

Charity was stunned when her landlady called one day and informed her she was leaving Charity the house in her will.

May 5

"Someday I'll retire and write my memoirs."

Charity contemplated that writing her memoirs would probably end up being a more or less verbatim report of her years at the Academy, with a few incidents from Andrew's life, especially his teen years, thrown in.

She was thinking about all this during lunch detention. (Andrew always laughed when she commented she had detention "Oh, mom, what did you do?")

Danny was filling in a detention slip/essay for committing an act of disrespect to a staff member. "Dis to staff" was the verbal abbreviation, understood by everyone at the Academy. "Why did you do this?" the slip queried. (Danny had been accused of leaving class without permission, as well.) "I didn't want to smell that perfume" he wrote. Apparently he had commented, in his notoriously rude way, on his opinion of a staff member's perfume, which was negative. "I couldn't stand it!" he commented. "It was too strong!"

"Besides," he said, sounding sad, something Danny never sounded like, "I'm not coming back. Today's my last day. It doesn't matter what I do, I can't succeed here anyway. All the teachers hate me."

Charity looked up at him, feeling bad. Most of them did. He was so hateful and obnoxious most of the time, she didn't think he cared what teachers thought of him. But this was too much.

"Danny" she said gently, "I can't speak for all the teachers, but I don't hate you. It's your behavior a lot of the time I don't like, but I don't hate you." She realized when she said it that it was true. She didn't know if he believed it or not, but he was extraordinarily well-behaved for the rest of detention.

That's why I'm here, she thought, these little moments that happen in between teaching.

Yes, her memoirs would no doubt be taken over by the kids at the Academy.

May 7

Charity felt discouraged. It wasn't just the weather, which was unnaturally cold for May, even for the region she lived in. It wasn't just the lack of money. It wasn't just having her second lunch duty of the week, and tutoring (for extra pay) after school, meaning she had no break all day. She was, she realized, depressed. Her depression wasn't a do-nothing-all-day-but-complain-and-feel-bad depression, like Felipe's, it was a plodding-one-foot-in-front-of-the-other-same-old-thing-over-and-over-what-good-is-it-anyway depression. So what if she worked all day, including lunch duty, tutoring after school, and a massage or two after that? She still couldn't make ends meet. People like Felipe, at times like this, made her livid. How dare he be a lily of the field, who neither toiled nor spun, when it was her toiling and spinning that kept them both going? Not very charitable, she realized, but she wished she could for once assume some of that attitude of entitlement. She certainly put enough effort out in the course of the day to feel entitled to some return for her investment.

Maybe letting go and trusting the same God who cared for the lilies of the field to care for her was all that she was lacking.

May 8

The next morning, Charity forewent feeding the dog and making her lunch and gave herself a soak in the tub instead. As she soaked, she allowed herself to let all the soreness, emotional too, go out of her and into the water. She allowed her thoughts to wander. She did not remember her dreams of the night before, and she did not permit herself to feel dread about the coming work day. She did not dwell on yesterday's disgust, despair, and aggravation, which led to a nasty argument with Felipe the Fieldlily.

Instead, she allowed what thoughts that would float up out of her unconscious, and one thought made her sit up straight in the tub.

She knew, because she remembered, what her younger sister's first word was. It was airplane ("airpane," with pointing to the sky.) She knew, because it was a family story, what her older brother's first word was: light. She did not know what her own first word was. Wasn't that a bit strange, she thought, to know her siblings first words and not her own? What did that say about her family? What did it say about her place in that family? She decided to call her mother and ask what it was. Her mother should remember that, shouldn't she?

She didn't. "I don't know, but I'll think about it, Charity. Maybe I have it written down somewhere. I'll look, and let you know."

When several weeks went by, and she hadn't heard from her mother about it, she asked her again. "I just don't remember."

"Well, why don't you try now?" Charity suggested.

"You were crazy about your daddy, so I'll bet your first word was daddy or da-da. Yes, I'm sure that's what it must have been," Charity's mother said.

Charity felt willing to compromise on "da-da" as her first word. She had been crazy about her father, and she called him "daddy" not father or any other variation. Later, when she was older, "dad," but that was as formal as it got. She always suspected she was his favorite child. He was always there for her.

"Da-da" had been Andrew's first word, too. Followed closely by cat, and he used them interchangeably for a while.

Charity liked that they shared a common verbal link as infants.

May 10

Charity began Saturday, her day off, with many plans. The weather continued to be too cool and cloudy for half of them. On call at the hotel health club, by 10:30 it looked as thought that wasn't going to happen, at least. Fieldlily got up, complained he hadn't slept enough, (he was forever complaining about sleep: it wasn't enough, it was interrupted, it wasn't restful.) This morning he couldn't blame anyone. Charity hadn't gotten up at the usual 6:30 (Fieldlily always claimed it was six o'clock) and Andrew had slept over at a friend's house. The cats had been quiet. So he couldn't blame anyone, he had just awakened and couldn't go back to sleep. He had breakfast and then went back to bed, and promptly fell asleep.

Charity reviewed her list of plans, and began to feel sulky. It required some phone calls, a lot of running around, and first of all getting dressed, which she couldn't do without going into the bedroom and waking up Fieldlily, who, if he would only go to bed at a decent hour (he was usually up until 1:00 or 2:00 because when he complained he wasn't rested and couldn't sleep, he usually went back to sleep until late morning and he wasn't tired until 2:00 am..) wouldn't need to sleep the morning away.

It was Mother's Day week-end, chances were some fool at the hotel would want a Mother's Day massage and she would be called and begged by Sophia (who would strongly suggest to the guest that since it was a lot to ask the masseuse to come in for just one appointment that she should leave a large tip) to come in for one hour appointment and the whole day would be wasted. Damn. She was a mother, it was her day too, why couldn't she have one day out of the week-end where someone considered her wants?

May 12

Charity made a list of her fears:

1. She was afraid of being poor, really poor, abjectly poor.
2. She was afraid of dying of a terrible lingering disease, incurable cancer or valvular heart disease.
3. She was afraid of being thought ridiculous. She was afraid of losing her intellectual faculties.
4. She was afraid of growing old and all the consequent slowing and lessening of her abilities. She was afraid of developing Alzheimer's.
5. She was afraid of losing Andrew to drugs, or illness, or a car accident. She was afraid for Andrew's spirit. Would he become a compassionate, sensitive, caring, committed-to-helping-the-earth-and-others-adult? Would he be healthy, intact, humane, strong? Able to resist the temptations to become the opposite? Had she done her job as a parent well?

Charity realized most of these fears were unfounded and not even based on reality. Yet she didn't want to be, as Fieldlily often accused her of being, "in denial" about reality. Life was hard, sometimes, and often unfair.

May 13

"Hey, Rob, how're you gonna run three businesses on an eighth grade education?" Dave asked.

Rob, a dreamer, had been bragging about what he was going to do with his life. Dave, a realist, didn't like the way Rob was always avoiding class work. The work program supervisor had just liberated Rob from class. It had been a stressful day, and Charity was happy to see him go. She had been listening to kids argue about assignments, discipline, and their lives in general all day.

After he finished his work (he always finished early, and earned grades in the 90's) Dave asked if he could look at a video. Charity's room adjoined the video library so she allowed him to choose a video. She was curious what he would choose. She figured that most of the videos were ok; they were educational, chosen by the teaching staff. Still, some of them looked questionable. To her surprise and delight, he chose a documentary on ancient Rome, and sat, fascinated, the entire remainder of the period.

Charity often wondered what Dave was doing here at all. He was so well-behaved and such a mature voice of reason.

May 14

It had been a rough two days at the Academy. The kids were getting spring fever and their way of getting it was to become loud, mouthy, aggressive and defiant.

It was a relief to sign out for part of the afternoon and drive up the hill to the high school that Andrew attended for their literary and art magazine opening. It was held in the auditorium and when Charity walked in, loud "techno" music was playing, strobe lights were flashing on stage and the kids were walking around in clothes reminiscent of the 60's and 70's, when Charity went to high school. It was like a gigantic flashback. After refreshments were served and magazines purchased, the readings began. Andrew read 4th. When his name was announced, he walked out on stage looking completely at ease. There were claps and cheers for him. He took the microphone and explained he was reading a poem that was untitled, he had just begun it last week, and it was therefore unfinished. Then, in a clear voice, he read a poem about an oak tree's life, compared it to human life and made some deep observations about life and nature. He looked out at the audience once or twice, blinked a bit at the spotlight, and ended. It could stand as a completed poem right where he left it.

Charity was moved almost to tears. She had aspired to writing poetry and had begun at about Andrew's age, 16 or 17, but nothing she wrote then was as impressive as this. And so relaxed on stage! Who was this creature she had spawned? He was her son, after all. Charity slipped out to go back to the Academy, thinking she wasn't such a bad parent after all. Not bad, at all.

May 15

Whew! It had been quite a day with Fieldlily.

It began when Charity was getting dressed. Since it was her day to escort a group of students to the Farm, she put on blue jeans, her only pair of jeans, cleaned for this purpose. Since she had gained a bit of weight, and since the jeans had just come out of the dryer, they were a snug fit. She put on a longish, long sleeved tee-shirt to cover them.

Fieldlily had a fit: "Those pants are too tight! And that shirt! It's too snug! It looks like a mini-skirt! Why didn't you allow time to plan for something different?"

Charity had expected something like this. "Look, Felipe, we have to go to the Farm today. This is my only pair of jeans. I have one other pair of pants and they are reasonably good. I can't afford a new pair of pants. I can't mess up my only good pair of pants. Why can't you just let me be?"

Charity deferred slightly even though it made her late by changing her shirt to a flannel one that was looser. "Any better?" she asked.

"Somewhat," said Fieldlily, "but I can still see your butt."

"Well, I do have one, big deal," said Charity, flying down the stairs, too late to even cry.

She drove down the road angry, angry, angry.

When she arrived home, Fieldlily came outside and jumped in the car conspiratorially.

"I just want to tell you the chronology" he said "about Andrew. He's ok, by the way."

"What?" said Charity, beginning to feel alarmed.

"There was a message on the machine. Andrew wasn't in school today. He needs a note to be readmitted. I know how to do it, so I saved the message. When I came back home later, the machine wasn't even blinking, and there was another message after it, so Andrew must have tried to erase the message. He could have erased my message. I think he should be punished for it."

"What?" said Charity, "this is confusing. What did the message say? Did you talk to him?"

"I asked if there were any important messages, so he wouldn't know I was accusing him and he said he hadn't listened to the machine at all! Why should you be confused?"

So Charity talked to Andrew.

"Yes, mom. I didn't feel good today. I didn't want to go to school. I wasn't sick, I just didn't feel like being around people. I did check the machine. I'm sorry."

Charity talked to her son about it for a while, telling him he could have said something that morning and asking if he was depressed. He felt better, he said, he just wanted a clear day and a clear head.

Later, he apologized to Fieldlily for lying about checking the answering machine. Fieldlily didn't shout, he merely asked Andrew to think about why he had lied. When he left the room, he turned to Charity.

"It's a miracle."

"What is?"

"It's a miracle that you never think Andrew is doing things. Like the phone card. He knew who had it, who was using it."

As a matter of fact, he did not. He had known one person who had been called illegally, without authorization, and he had called and demanded to know who might have called, trying to find out who was using the card. That was it, and he had been as angry and upset as Charity was.

At this point, Charity was furious. "You don't like the way I manage my son. You don't like the way I manage time, always asking me why I didn't plan for things in the morning, why I didn't realize I was short on time." She thought. "You don't like the way I manage money, always saying didn't I know this bill was coming? Why, if you don't like the way I manage anything, don't you try to earn some money to manage? Why, since you don't like my time economy in the mornings, don't you try getting up and helping, instead of lying in bed and leveling criticism at me?" She thought of saying.

She wondered what Fieldlily would do if she said this out loud or if she coolly suggested, "If you don't like things here, as they are, why don't you just leave?"

Otherwise, the rest of the day had presented opportunities to help others in a small way. Charity had long felt that if she couldn't help her fellow human beings on a grand, global level, that she could at least do one small thing for one person everyday, if the need presented itself, and not even mention it. That was important. Just try, quietly, to make a small difference for the better, whereever you could, and don't boast about it. Just do it.

Today, there were two opportunities. She saw a colleague walking home after work and offered him a ride. She had an appointment, for which she needed to withdraw money from the bank teller machine, and when she pulled up to the bank, there was someone in front of her. It turned out to be another colleague, who was unfamiliar with the ATM, and finally asked for her help. She found out what transaction he wanted, pushed the right buttons, he thanked her and was on his way.

Charity felt grateful she was able to help two people in one day. If you can help people, you were rich, even if you had little or no money.

May 19

The 8th grade:

"I'm not working. I'll take the zero."

"Why do we have so much work?"

"Can't I use the computer for this?"

"I did too look up more than one word, I looked up five, don't you feel dumb!"

"This chair is killing my back."

"What time is this class over?"

"Can I use the bathroom?"

"What does jovial mean?"

"After this I'm not doing any more work!"

"Can you call my social worker?"

"Can you call the nurse?"

"Can I go to the office?"

"I was just singing a song!"

"I need a new workbook!"

"He's instigating me. Give him a fine."

"How do you spell pudgy?"

"I'll punch you in the grill, you keep bothering me!"

"I only have fifteen minutes left to play on the computer!"

"I'm just playin' with you!"

May 20

Charity tried to give where and how she could. She invariably stopped and gave a dollar to the volunteer fire companies that had tag days. She sent money to two religious groups that she felt an affinity to, Unity and the Little Flower Society. She gave money to the veterans. (This past Saturday when driving to the hotel, she gave money to the Vets and received a pen in return - one that commemorated Viet Nam Vets. Charity felt doubly happy that she had put in her dollar there. Viet Nam was her generation and she felt the wounds from that war had never healed. She was glad the Vet's organizations were supporting Viet Nam Vets - so many other government agencies had turned their backs on them, wanting to forget their mistakes and any reminders of them - even those that gave their lives, a limb, their health, or their emotional well-being in the process.) Charity had even paid off the balance of a private loan from the Academy that her former husband, Andrew's father, had out-standing. She bought library raffle tickets, she supported bake sales.

All these were done quietly, without mention and no desire for recognition. Charity felt it was the only true charitable way. Even though money, or its constant short supply, was often an issue for her, she nevertheless gave where and when she could, even if it was only one dollar here and there. She had never stopped to add it up, and she would have been pleasantly surprised to find that she actually in a year's time, made a sizable contribution toward the betterment of her community, and the world at large.

May 22

Charity had always wanted to write, or rather, to be considered a writer. In fact, she wrote nearly everyday, but her dream was to be a published, acclaimed writer. So when she had a chance to attend an "Arts in Therapies" conference and earn continuing education credits from the Academy (they were expected to keep honing their skills, not that they received pay increases for it like some public schools) of course, she would attend the writing workshops. She taught English, to adolescents designated "emotionally disturbed," so the writing session would be perfectly justified. Things seldom fell into place so smoothly, especially in Charity's life.

At the conference, several people mentioned what had started them on successful writing careers. One speaker mentioned journal writing had been the initial path for many writers. This speaker went on to say she had begun keeping a diary at about age ten. This caused a memory bell to ring in Charity's mind. Her mother, whom Charity had, of late, been more angry with than not, had started Charity's journal writing career at about age ten, when she gave Charity a diary in her Christmas stocking. She had further encouraged Charity's writing by giving her a diary every

Christmas for some time after that. She had saved Charity's childhood stories, written in school and out. She had helped Charity to think of herself as a writer. Her mother hadn't encouraged her in some ways that Charity wished she had, but her writing was encouraged, and Charity just realized, today, that she owed her mother a thank-you for that. She decided to call her to tell her so.

May 24

Charity suspected Fieldlily of reading her journals. More than suspected - she knew he had read some of her older journals, ones she had kept before she knew him. He had gone through them, systematically, and had the audacity to confront her about things in them, things having nothing whatsoever to do with him, and very little to do anymore with her. How dare he! Didn't he realize what a violation that was? Didn't he realize what an avenue of release he was cutting off for her? Because when she found out, she was loathe to keep a journal for a long time, and that had been her path of self-exploration, of working through psychological and emotional problems. Didn't he realize, for God's sake, that people change? That the Charity of ten years ago, the one who wrote in the journals he had read, had evolved? No. He had confronted the Charity of ten years ago, not even seeing the Charity of today. He, who prided himself on being so astute, so intuitive, so perceptive. Perhaps it was because he had changed so little over the years, he seemed to be stuck in his own teen-age rite of passage, a still birth from adolescent to adult. And now, at nearly 40, he was having a "mid-life crisis." It must be awful to be stuck in adolescence and having a middle age crisis at the same time. She hoped nothing of the sort would happen to Andrew. She hoped he could successfully navigate his adolescent passage.

A thought occurred to her that maybe that is what a mid life crisis in men was all about. Most of them never made it out of adolescence. It wasn't a second adolescence that was sparked by aging; it was a prolonged, atrophied adolescence that was causing all the problems.

May 25

Charity found it ironic and some what predictable that, now, she had decided to try writing that a dozen things presented themselves as more immediate and interesting to her. She had always wanted to be a writer - this was the acid test. Did she really want to? Enough to commit to writing something everyday?

This morning, a Sunday, and the middle of four days off from the Academy, plenty of time to write, Charity found herself suddenly wanting to clean out her closet. She never wanted to even go near her closet, usually. Or scrub the mildew off the bathroom ceiling, or call her sister, whom she almost never wanted to talk to, and it was a long-distance, i.e. costly, call. Or take the dog for a long walk, even though it was raining.

The phone rang. The hotel. It would be busy at the health club this afternoon due to the rain. Would she be available to come in?

Fieldlily got up, complaining of a headache that he attributed to their arguments of yesterday and the day before. Charity offered to rub his neck and shoulders, out of guilt and avoidance of writing.

What was this game she was playing with herself? Fear of success, or what?

She persisted and wrote anyway. Then she rubbed Fieldlily's neck.

May 26

Memorial Day, Charity thought, and used it to remember her family, those dead and those alive, but far away.

I need a vacation, she thought. Not just four days off from teaching school, with half of two of those days taken up with massage therapy, her other profession. Especially after a day like yesterday.

It was a rainy Sunday with a holiday the next day. "It should be busy." Sophia had said when she called that morning. "Marney is already booked for the afternoon and Anna is leaving at 3:00." When Charity arrived at 2:45 she found her last three appointments had canceled. Oh, well, I'm here now, maybe the two left will leave a nice tip. "You may pick up one or two drop-ins" Sophia consoled.

Appointment number one, named Esther, plopped herself down backwards on the table, complaining of her neck paining her. The entire rest of the session - mercifully only a half hour! - she proceeded to be a pain in Charity's neck. Oh, work more on my neck. Oh, you didn't do my fingers. (Charity had.) Oh, do my fingers more. My lower back, could you do that again? And on and on. When Sophia poked her face in the door and announced her next appointment was there, Charity was relieved. All finished she said sweetly to Esther appointment number one. Esther did not leave a tip.

Appointment number two, also an Esther, began by introducing herself, demanding Charity's name, and declaring she had massages "in the city" twice a week, Charity could go hard, she was used to it. She immediately asked, once in the cubicle, what oil Charity used. When Charity falteringly replied, mentioning the arnica that she had found so useful for sore muscles, Esther the 2nd cut her off and thrust a bottle into her hand. "Well, I have olive oil. Use it!" (Huh! Probably rancid Italian olive oil, Charity thought with contempt.) "Don't you have tiger balm?" Esther II bellowed.

The hour (sigh, a whole hour with this hellion!) did not improve. "Go harder! I can take it!" macho Esther demanded. She insisted on lying on her back, even though Charity began working on people's backs first. "What technique are you employing?" Esther demanded.

After Charity had finished Esther's hands, Esther had chosen to share with her that her fingers, especially her ring fingers, bothered her, especially after last night. "All the salt in those olives!" Why didn't you tell me this before? Charity silently wondered, because she had asked at the start, when she could get a word in, what was bothering Esther today? And why eat salty olives if you know they bother you? Again, to herself. Out loud, Charity asked if Esther wanted her to do her hands again. "No, just go on," Esther replied grumpily. "Harder."

When Esther turned over, Charity began to work on her neck. Harder. "Ouch!" Esther yelped. "Too hard."

Charity Begins at Home 51

Make up your mind, Charity grumbled to herself. She tried to more gently work Esther's neck, but Esther finally said, "Just go on. Forget my neck." When Charity placed a small pillow on the side of her head Esther resisted. "I hate anything under my head!" she said. "It's just a little one, to relieve the pressure on your neck," Charity had reassured her. "Try it and see if it helps." It did. Half hour to go (!!)

Charity vowed after this to follow her instincts and insist people start out the way she, Charity, asked them to, the way she had been trained, a technique far superior than most.

When Charity was finally at Esther's legs (the last leg, Charity thought, my last leg) she noticed the varicose veins. Ah ha! Charity thought. My instincts to go lighter were right. One should never go deeply into varicose veins - the risk of causing a blood clot to break loose and lodge elsewhere (lungs, heart) were too great. Also, if Esther had only listened to her request to be face down on the table, Charity would have seen the veins first and not felt pressured to work more deeply than she felt she should.

"Ouch! That hurts!" Esther mumbled as Charity gently rubbed her last leg. Charity went on to her feet. "You know," what now? Charity thought "my toes bother me." As Charity dug in to the last little toe, Esther said, "Actually it's only my middle toe."

As she left, Esther remarked to Sophia how excellent the masseuse was. She did not leave a tip.

The third and last half hour was pleasant. "This is so relaxing," she commented once. Charity felt agitated from Esther the Terrible; she was probably working rougher than she needed to, she realized. She eased up. Number three did not leave a tip, either.

   I really need a vacation, Charity thought. Not just four days off, where I work part of that time, a real vacation. Free from worry, money concerns, complaints, cleaning, and duties. A real vacation. Even a day away. A vacation. Away.

   Early the next day, Memorial Day, the phone rang. It was Sophia. Anna had not checked in, she had four appointments, could Charity come in? (Sophia knew she always needed the money.) All right, Charity sighed inwardly, I'll come.

May 27

While she worked, Charity let her mind wonder. She wasn't as out of sorts as yesterday and today's clients were a nicer group. Not big tippers, mind you, but not so demanding. So Charity worked automatically and let her mind go over various concerns. Which bills to pay with the check from the hotel? She wished she could pay one big bill off entirely - her MasterCard - but it always seemed like she ended up putting a little here and there to keep creditors at bay for three more weeks. Car insurance was due. Damn!

And her house. Such a mess all the time. It didn't used to be that way. When she had moved in at first, she had kept it neat, inside and out, once she had arranged things the way she wanted them. She had even, at one time, when she had shared the house with the Golfer, hired someone to clean it regularly. While Charity felt the cleaner did a half hearted job, she did it regularly and once she was gone, Charity realized how much better a job the cleaner did than Charity herself was able to do! But now she couldn't afford that, she couldn't afford to hire a lawn cutter, she needed to get the old lawn mower fixed, she couldn't afford to - her fortunes had definitely slipped. She didn't like living this way, in squalor, she thought of it. She wished she had more energy and more organizational skills, so she could keep a neater, cleaner house. Fieldlily was no help. Oh, he did the dishes once in a while but never anything else. What did he do all day? Charity wondered. Sit and worry about his depression, his allergies, how he hated "this area," how badly Charity managed Andrew, her money, her life? Fieldlily couldn't vacuum. He was allergic to house dust and house mites and vacuuming was the worst for putting them into the air. He couldn't mow grass. He was allergic to grasses and pollens of all kinds. "My mother would call this house unkempt," he had once remarked. "Get a job," Charity had thought to herself.

In desperation, she sent Andrew out to cut down the tallest grass with a hand scythe.

May 29

Charity awoke at 5:15, one hour before the alarm. She hadn't fallen asleep until 11:30, even though she was tired. She had been unable to sleep much the night before, either, which is why she had been tired all day. Not falling asleep right away and waking up just before she was rested and not enough before the alarm to make it worth while trying to get back to sleep - sometimes it took a while - was not usual for Charity. So why be cursed now?

Too many things on her mind. The Academy had switched assistants on her, again, and this new one was not only unable, she was unwilling and argumentative as well! So it had been a rough first day back from a long weekend. Andrew's father was on the warpath. He had a habit of calling Andrew or Charity about some supposed grievance, yelling irrationally, and hanging up before anyone could answer his unreal, demanding, abusive diatribe. When he called and Fieldlily picked up the phone, Fieldlily would tell him, before he had a chance to blather, that he couldn't call there with that attitude and, if he did, Fieldlily would call the police on him for harassment. (Bless Fieldlily! Charity thought. He's good for some things!)

Andrew's father did not appreciate this, needless to say. He was used to having unlimited access to vent his rage on his victims. He was constantly threatening, when thwarted, to have his cousin, a lawyer, write a letter or press charges, (Against Fieldlily? Charity? Andrew?) claiming that not being able to rant indiscriminately against Charity was in violation of their divorce agreement. He claimed she was not communicating and not allowing him to communicate valuable information about Andrew. Charity wondered just what part of their divorce agreement entitled him to be abusive to her for years after the divorce. She wondered just what information she was blocking when she refused to hear a litany of her "sins" for the past fifteen years. She wondered what made him think she was not communicating when he hung up the phone on her after one of his tirades. She wondered why he thought his unchecked abusive behavior was acceptable and not in need of restraint and why Fieldlily's action of merely cutting off his tirades was?

The more she thought about it, the more Andrew's father reminded her of the wickedly prideful man in the Psalms whose ways were grievous.

"As for all his enemies, he puffeth at them."

Charity could see him puffething. She prayed that God would set her, Andrew, and Fieldlily "in safety from he that puffeth."

The language of the King James Version of the Bible never failed to satisfy Charity. The same Psalms in the New English Bible read,

"His ways are devious… He scoffs at all restraint." and "I say the Lord will place him in the safety for which he longs."

Something got lost in that translation, something ineffable. Charity preferred the imagery of the version that puffeth.

May 31

On Saturday, Charity awoke early. Rain was predicted, but for now it was beautifully clear and finally warm.

She went out on the deck and sat quietly in the sun. The deck was raised, so one could access it from the kitchen door. The house, an old lock tender's cottage (the lock complete with old rusty car thrown in it in the back, adjacent to the river) was built into a sloping hillside, so the ground floor was open to the back, and the front door led into the second level. So the deck was actually on the second storey, with a huge evergreen tree hanging over it, and a hawthorn tree next to it on the other side. Charity loved it. It was like having a tree house. From the deck, you could look through the woods and see the river flowing by.

It had been hell-week at the Academy. Charity's new assistant was not working out. She had a princess attitude toward what she would or would not do. She refused, for instance, to be present during homeroom, and spent a day and a half wandering out, without a word, avoiding it, taking an hour and a half for lunch. "Where's Ms. Wood?" the kids kept asking. "I don't know," Charity would reply each time. Oh, well, the kids seemed to say, it doesn't matter. You're the constant in our lives. And she was. The kids were the reason Charity stayed on at the Academy. The pay was low, so low that Charity fell further into debt with every year she was there. How could she work so hard and try to be so thrifty, and still not make ends meet? She sometimes wondered. What was she doing wrong? But even when the kids were mouthy, aggressive, and seemingly hopeless delinquents, Charity felt that there were moments of truth where they could be reached and helped, if there was anyone there to try. Charity strove to be the one who tried. She might fail nine times, but get through the tenth, and she refused to give up hope.

Sometimes, with a somewhat cynical sense of humor, Charity imagined clubs like the ones she remembered from school, "Future Teachers of America," etc. They could start the "Future Criminals of America" or the Burglars Club. The Car Club could demonstrate ways to hotwire troublesome luxury cars, or suggest which stolen parts brought the greatest profit on the streets. The Jailhouse Lawyers could instruct ways to argue their own and other's cases in court, for a fee, of course. And there was always the "Future Drug Dealers of America," sort of a self-help group. Charity sighed, wondered if she was becoming too cynical, and got up to find paper to work out a new budget.

June 1

It was the third anniversary of Charity's marriage to Fieldlily. As Charity reflected on this, early in the morning (Fieldlily being characteristically still asleep.) She thought that it felt longer. Much longer. A lifetime. After only a few months of marriage, no, actually after only a few months of their relationship, Fieldlily lost the job he had held for over a year (probably some kind of record for him, Charity snorted.) He hadn't been able to collect unemployment and he had at first seemed willing, eager, even, to find another job. Meanwhile, he began the first of religious initiations and the beginning of a search that continued to this day, for a true spiritual leader.

When he finally found a very part-time job, late in the summer, Charity was pleased. Any extra income was helpful.

Meanwhile, his car died and although it could have been revived for the cost of a down payment on a new one, they decided to lease a new car and sell the old one to a friend that Fieldlily owed money to. Fieldlily's salary would cover the monthly cost of the leased car.

The car could not be leased, for some reason and they were persuaded to buy it, since living with one car and two jobs was becoming impossible. The monthly payment was twice, nearly, what the lease payment would have been and shortly after this Fieldlily lost his job. Since he had held it for over five months, however, he collected unemployment benefits this time around. There was some delay and when he finally collected his first check, it was in a lump sum which he used for another initiation, one that would enable him to practice this religion and earn money doing so. He felt he'd found his spiritual teacher at last.

He hadn't. He was disillusioned. He continued his spiritual search, he gave up doing consultations, and he never found, or even looked for, another job. Fieldlily seemed to see working as some sort of occupational hazard to his spiritual and intellectual life. It had been a long three years.

Oh well, Charity thought, with Andrew leaving for college next year or maybe this one, she'd need somebody to look after and worry about. As if all those boys at the Academy weren't enough!

June 3

Fieldlily was on the rampage again. He was enraged that Charity should have any contact with Andrew's father. Since Charity didn't usually want to (Andrew's father raged, as well, and called it "communication") she couldn't understand why she had to have stereo tantrums.

Because Fieldlily was livid about some "conversation" that took place over a year ago, and Charity had explained once what she had said, and Fieldlily had only heard the first word, not waiting for clarification, and Charity had firmly said, "That's not what I said and if you didn't hear it, it doesn't mean I didn't say it," and said again for clarity, what she had said the first time, and Fieldlily had acknowledged that he heard it the second time, but wanted to belabor the first statement, why Charity couldn't possibly have clarified it then because it wasn't, "in his memory," and Charity had refused to allow him to belabor it, saying that she had said what she had to say, because all this occurred, and Charity would not permit him to vent his spleen at her, saying she was going to change her clothes and plant the lilies of the valley, because she did that, Fieldlily chose something else to erupt about: not only was Charity in her black dance pants (too thin! Too shiny! Too revealing if she bent over!) Not only that but she was wearing them in front of the house! Two years ago, when she wore red boots in front of the house (to shovel the snow that he was unable to shovel because the year before he had hurt his back shoveling snow) someone with a plow on his truck had actually stopped and offered to plow the driveway for five dollars. Fieldlily took this as a flirtation on the plower's part which was elicited by the sight of her red boots. Charity took it as someone wanting to make an extra five dollars wherever he could, and since she didn't have five dollars, she had said no thanks.

Now Fieldlily was upset because Charity did not want to have that obsessive argument again and he wanted to jump down her throat about something tonight. Why?

The reason was simple. Fieldlily was alternately depressed and angry. He was in the house all day so he was also bored. He would sleep at odd hours, due to depression and allergies. Consequently, the tension would build to a point that he found intolerable and he would pick a fight with Charity and blame her "miscommunication" for it and when he whipped himself into peak frenzy, using her actions or behavior or words as an excuse, he would ultimately break something to relieve the tension. Usually it was something of his that cost a fair amount of money and that, naturally, Charity had originally purchased for him, since of course, he neither toiled nor spun. "See what you made me do?" he would then shriek at her. "You know I don't care about material things! You know I wouldn't have to break things if you would only communicate!"

This time, actually for some time, Charity was having none of it. "Since you've been breaking things and punching holes in the walls since you were a teenager, I fail to see how this behavior is in any way my doing. And furthermore screaming and breaking things is about as miscommunicative as it comes. It's worse than silence, which I prefer," she said coolly.

Amazing. "Her miscommunication." Fieldlily and Andrew's father were like two peas in a pod.

Tomorrow Fieldlily had his bimonthly appointment with his counselor. Charity often wondered why he bothered to go. He never seemed to bring any of the anxiety, anger or depression up to the therapist. He seemed to focus on "telling on" her, and emphasizing his excellent, rational thought and how skilled he was at expressing his feelings and communicating in general, getting the therapist to agree and affirm this, sort of a building-up-his-self-esteem session. At least that's what Charity, who was paying for the sessions, could gather.

It was unbelievable. Did abusive people actually think they were behaving rationally and justifiably and were therefore doing nothing wrong? Charity realized that, no, they really didn't see anything wrong with their behavior. They actually thought it was ok.

Fieldlily, Andrew's father, they could be cruel and hurtful and not even think they were out of control or even out of line. What was wrong with them? What was wrong with her, choosing to marry two such verbally and emotionally abusive men?

June 5

Most bizarrely, when Andrew's father asked Andrew what was bothering him and he had replied that Fieldlily was arguing with his mom, his father had said to let his mom know that if she needed any help at all, if she ever wanted to get a divorce, he would help her. This was after threatening to have his cousin, a lawyer, write a letter about Fieldlily's supposed "harassment" of hanging up the phone and saying not to call there, call on Andrew's own phone. He kept asking Andrew, "Did she get the letter yet?" And when he could get through to Charity at the Academy he would ask her, "Did you get the letter yet? You'll be getting a letter; I'm not putting up with this violation of our divorce agreement!" Charity wondered just which clause in their divorce agreement specified that she or Andrew had to listen to his verbal abuse. She said as much and he hissed something unintelligible and hung up. No letter ever arrived.

June 6

"Order your lives in charity, upon that model of charity which Christ showed to us, when he gave himself up on our behalf." Ephesians 5:2

Charity was becoming slightly obsessed with biblical quotations containing her name. Was her destiny written in one of them? In all? None?

What should she do with conversations such as she had just had with Anne, a person at work that she essentially liked, but who inadvertently had offended her? It was inadvertent, for Anne was a devout Christian, who truly tried, Charity believed, to live her life without offending her fellow persons. The most obvious charitable thing was to forget it and let it go. She didn't mean anything by it. But was that the most charitable thing? It was erroneous thinking, and harmful. Harmful to all women, which of course meant harmful to Anne herself. Wouldn't it be the most charitable to tell Anne and save her from self-destructive thinking?

June 7

Whew! Another Saturday. The weeks just whizzed by, Charity thought. The weeks flew by, the bills went unpaid, the garbage piled up, the grass grew from knee to waist high. The lilacs in front hadn't bloomed this year. Why? The peonies never bloomed. The hosta directly in front never did either, and the juniper bush had died. What was it? Was it poor drainage, acid soil, not much sun, too much rain? All her neighbors' flowers bloomed to perfection.

The house felt damp, musty; smelled moldy and dirty. The vacuum never seemed to take care of the dust or pet hair. The septic seemed to be leaking worse.

That had its merits. When Charity had exchanged plants with Grace at the Academy, (Charity gave her bergamot and lemon balm for burning bush and lily of the valley) Grace had exclaimed over how large the lemon balm and bergamot were. Charity immediately offered more, "I have it to spare," she said, "it's run rampant out back." Grace said, "It must be a protected area." "No," said Charity, "I think it has to do with the septic leaking."

Grace looked disbelieving as if Charity was making a joke. Charity left it that way. She was known for her skewed, wry sense of humor.

When she related her latest fight with Fieldlily to her therapist, the therapist had worked with her to come up with a plan to cope with him and actually help him in the long run. Charity had agreed that this was a good idea and felt capable of attempting it. Then she had said, "but I have this fantasy of what I really want to happen. I want him to take the old car which needs replacing but I can't afford to and it keeps running, so I'll keep driving it, I keep hoping he'll drive off in it in one of his rages, not in the new car and he'll be out of control and crash it and die."

It seemed like the perfect, neat solution to both problems, the old car and Fieldlily. Charity was a Virgo, after all.

Somewhat taken aback, the therapist said how Charity probably would feel very badly if something like that happened, etc.

Charity had smiled and replied, "Every cloud has a silver lining."

June 9

And indeed, every cloud does. Charity reminded herself of this when, the next day, she heard the news that Jason, a friend of Fieldlily's and then hers, a young friend, sort of like a foster son or nephew, had tried to kill himself. He had realized, before it was too late, that he didn't want to, after all, and came out of it, and called them at 2:00 am. Fieldlily, up as usual, took the call. The next morning Charity mentioned they had better bring him over to their house and look out for him a while. When kids at the Academy threatened or attempted suicide they were immediately put "on eyeball" and kept under close supervision. Jason was older but Charity felt the situation called for the same action. Fieldlily initially said no, remember the last time he stayed with us, he makes me crazy, remember? Charity thought, "who are you kidding makes you crazy, you're crazy already," but she thought of what it would mean to have another person around, another dependent, as Jason didn't have a job and, of course, neither did Fieldlily.

When they went to see Jason, Fieldlily suddenly relented and it was Charity who was feeling her doubts. Regardless, they brought Jason home with them and Charity set him up in the guest room/living room.

The next morning she felt cranky. After getting Andrew off to school she went around doing her morning chores, getting ready for her day at the Academy. She opened her devotional book, as she did every morning and read the wrong chapter, which happened to be completely apropos to her mood and the situation. It was all about extending charity, not meanness, when called for and in so doing reaping blessings on your own behalf. Charity smiled. She felt better. There were truly no accidents.

June 10

Charity made a list of all the things she hated:

Religious fanatics, especially Christians who are convinced of the evil of all others, even other Christians if they didn't believe and practice exactly as they themselves did.

Hypocrites, especially rageaholics like Andrew's father and Fieldlily, who condemned the same actions in others.

Bill collectors and creditors who called her by her first name. (She often asked them, "Do I know you?" And when they said no, she would demand to know why they were being so familiar.)

Having to come home from a day at the Academy and do house cleaning. Fieldlily was there all day, doing precious little else, he couldn't pick up a mop or a dish rag once in a while?

Being called at work by creditors, her former husband, or just about anyone unless it was good news or an emergency.

Spending money - a sizable amount each month - for health insurance and still having to pay for tests, office visits, dental work, etc. She paid more than she was sure she'd ever spend on her own.

Calling it "life insurance" when it was really a "death benefit."

Working inside during the summer.

Driving in snowy, icy storms.

Worrying about skin cancer and other, lesser afflictions from being in the sun. The sun! She was a priestess to the sun in a past life, she was sure, and now to have to shun it?

Dealing with Andrew's perpetually ranting, arrogant, spiteful, hypocritical, in-denial father.

Anxiety about money, or situations in her life or Andrew's waking her up in the middle of the night and keeping her awake.

June 12

It was Charity's turn to do lunch duty for the day students at the Academy. She could be assigned to either accompany a pack of them to the dining room or to stay back in the "self - management" room for lunch detention. Today it was her turn to stay back for detention. There was only one student, Luis. Charity liked Luis, but he was a holy terror. It was hot today, so Luis was subdued, for Luis. "Hola! It's you!" He exclaimed when Charity walked in. Luis liked Charity because she spoke Spanish and it made him feel secure.

After they ate and Luis had finished his detention essay, he became restless. It was June and hot in the self-management room. "What should I do now?" Luis asked. Charity thought. In detention they weren't supposed to do anything except their essays and sit quietly, to ponder their misdoings, no doubt, she mused; not even read or write a letter, just sit, ponder, get restless, bored and think up more misbehaviors.

Charity thought some more. Luis was one of the younger students at the Academy and she taught the upper levels. "Why don't you sit in front of this fan and draw a picture?" she finally suggested. Bend the rules a little, she thought, he's the only one here and these kids need direction. "What should I draw?" Luis asked. "Draw your idea of a favorite pet," Charity said firmly. "Ok." He was engaged for some minutes before he looked up. Charity didn't speak, she'd let him discuss it or show her if he chose to. He did. "It's my pet dinosaur, Larry. I don't draw too well but here I am riding on his tail." Charity looked and said, "It looks just like a Tyrannosaurus Rex." "I'm going to finish," Luis continued, and talked as he drew, "Larry is singing, here's the microphone, and he's on Oprah, here's Oprah. How do you spell Oprah?"

Charity looked and was charmed. There was Oprah, in perfect proportion to Larry, the T. Rex, with TV lights. It was perfect. "It's for you," Luis announced.

June 13

Later that afternoon, Charity sat at her desk catching up on paperwork. Akeim, one of her homeroom students, came in, "look, Miss!" Charity was barely aware, so intent was she on her paperwork. "No, look!" She looked up and saw a small, what she assumed was rubber, lizard on her desk. Akeim clearly expected her to be startled. Or maybe he just wanted her to see it. "Is that real?" she asked. "Look," and Akeim gently stroked its head and coaxed it into his hand. It was real. "I'm putting it in my terrarium with my other salamander."

For the second time that day, Charity was charmed.

Charity had nothing but contempt for people who cut down mature lilacs and called it "beautification." Or for those who pulled out into the street when they had a stop sign, blocking half the street, and impeding her progress when she had the right of way. This especially bothered her when the brakes on her car were bad. Or when people pulled out in front of her causing her to apply her brakes and then drove away very slowly. What was all the rush about before? Charity had contempt for people, let's be specific, men, who couldn't work because they were depressed. Charity had known a number of depressed women but all of them were still able to function, especially if they had children who needed caring for or to be supported financially. No woman Charity knew, including herself, used depression as an excuse not to work.

It was a good thing, too, because Charity needed to work every chance she got. Her stability and reliability had not only served her well on the job, they had served her well as a parent. Andrew was a calm, stable, strong and sensitive young man in part, great part, when you looked at his erratic, frenetic, unpredictable father, due to her influence.

June 18

Charity drove to her dance class. It was the Monday class, one that was held in a small private studio just outside of a small arts town near hers.

She was devoted to her dance classes and tried to take as many during the week as she could fit in and afford. The last few years she had studied dance with two teachers who were professional dancers and refugees from a modern dance troupe in the City. They were both dazzling dancers and also happened to be excellent teachers.

Still, this class troubled her. It was with the younger teacher and it wasn't as advanced as the older teacher's class, but Charity had trouble with it. She didn't like the choreography as well, usually, and she always felt like she was viewed as slow, nice but dumb, and somewhat repugnant. It wasn't the teacher's fault, it was just the way Charity felt, she couldn't help it. "It must be some emotional inadequacy on my part," she thought as she drove. Yet she rarely, if ever, felt that way in the more advanced, performing level class. Granted, she had studied with the older teacher for many more years, but it was more than familiarity. This teacher had an enthusiasm for the individual's diverse abilities, and encouraged them. They all said, "It's not about how high your leg is, it's how well you do it, how you carry yourself," but this teacher really meant it.

June 20

After being cold all spring, it was suddenly hot. Charity didn't do well in the heat. Classes at the Academy had been horrendous. Even more horrendous was the thought of classes all summer. The Academy, being a "residential school for troubled youth," ran a year round school program. It was rather European that way, except that the "summer holidays" weren't as long.

Charity's room, on the south side of the school building, was always stifling in the afternoons. Open windows invited bugs, which set off the kids like almost nothing else except maybe snakes. This year, since a new addition to the school was finally approved and begun, there would also be noise and dust. It figured, Charity thought, that when a new dormitory was being built, on the other side of the school, her room had been on that side. It figured, now that her room was across the hall, the construction was now on that side, too.

With the windows closed, it was unbearable. With them open, the noise made any verbal instruction impossible. There was, of course, no air conditioning. It was promised with the new addition that the cranky old furnace would be replaced and at the same time central air conditioning would be installed. Since at every turn the budget was being cut, Charity wasn't holding her breath. At any rate, there would be no AC this summer, only these enormous old fans that made a huge noise like an antique airplane, blew enormous gusts of wind around the small classroom and blew stacks of paper and small children out the windows if they happened to be open.

The kids would complain, "I don't wanna be here," and Charity would reply, "I don't want to either." That somehow always shocked them into momentary silence. Didn't all teachers just naturally want to be in the classroom all the time? If they didn't actually live there, didn't they want to? Charity didn't do well in the heat.

June 21

Charity knew the answer to Freud's question, "What do women want?"

They want to be left alone.

June 22

The heat continued. Charity was called in to work at the hotel health club on Saturday because Marney was elsewhere on her scheduled day and Charity had agreed to cover for her. Beastly hot to begin with outside, the massage area of the health club was always 20% hotter, due to poor planning. It backed onto the steam room, there was no ventilation, and the air conditioner did not work properly. Even with two fans going full blast it was brutally hot. Guests complained about it, the health club receptionist complained about it, Charity and the other massage therapists complained about it, to no avail. Charity steamed and dripped through a whole, long Saturday. When she got home and in the shower, she discovered she had a heat rash of all things. Charity did not do well in the heat.

June 23

The last day of the school year at the Academy. But not for long - summer session was just around the corner, less than two weeks away.

Charity was disturbed and she didn't know exactly why. She didn't want to work the summer, but she couldn't afford not to, and even if she could, it wasn't like she and Fieldlily ever took trips, or vacations, or did anything. If she could have afforded the time off and the expenses, Charity could have filled her summer with a number of things that interested her.

She'd begin with a week in Vermont studying the Alexander Technique. Ironically, this year the week fell at a time where it would have been intersession at the Academy, but Charity could no longer afford the tuition or room and board, all of which had increased considerably.

She then would go to Colorado, to a group for women who were interested in stimulating their own creativity, run by her therapist.

Then she would go to Italy to study and perform with her two modern dance teachers.

Then to South Dakota, to a workshop on the Rosebud Indian Reservation, about working with troubled youth, run by a Lakota psychologist, who was also an Episcopal priest. He had addressed her teacher's association group last year, and had made a lasting impression on Charity. He was so warm, compassionate, open, concise, practical and, dare she say it? loving, that Charity had wanted to leave the assembly when he did and follow him home, soaking up all the warmth and information that she could.

She would finish with a week at Cape Cod, visiting Andrew's grandparents and basking on the beach.

She would fill in the extra time by swimming, growing flowers and writing short stories about a woman who taught at a private school and danced and had one son and wrote and was concerned about money. But she'd leave out Fieldlily, making her character a single mother and she'd kill off her son's father, making her a widow and she'd add a few more pets. The nice thing about fiction was that you could rearrange the facts to suit yourself. Charity liked that.

"And above all these things, put on Charity, which is the bond of perfectness." - the King James Version of the Bible again. The bond of perfectness is Charity. She always knew it!

June 26

Andrew had failed math and needed to take it in summer school if he expected to take his senior year of high school at the local community college, also if he expected a regent's diploma... which he expected. Actually, which his father greatly expected and Charity did to a somewhat lesser degree. Having grown up and gone to undergraduate school in Ohio, Charity never really understood or accepted the "Regents Diploma" idea. School was school, why have all these levels for graduation diplomas? Why have an extra week of exams in June, when everyone was hot and cranky and just wanted to be out of school at last, students and teachers alike? For a statewide exam, surrounded by as much mystery and security measures as an international secret. It was as if the state of New York did not trust its teachers, which it expected to be overly trained and qualified (a masters degree required which could have qualified anyone to teach at a college somewhere else, but since it was a masters in education, it was also somehow woefully inadequate.) It was as if the state of New York had to step in like some paternalistic lord to oversee the final testing which teachers could most certainly handle constructing themselves!

Why not just offer a high school diploma and let the courses a student chose determine where he or she went after graduation? If college bound, the student took the courses required to enter the college of his or her choice. If job bound, they took skills courses to enable them to get the vocational training they needed. Why make it more difficult than it already was?

Of course Andrew was adamant. He would not go to summer school. He wanted to travel; he had a job. Andrew's father, never rational or subtle, was equally adamant that he would. He even took it one irrelevant, childish step further. It would be Andrew's punishment (he used the word "consequence") for all the supposed wrongs Andrew or Charity had ever done to him.

This was too much for Charity. She stepped in, calmly, strongly and formidably. They were in the high school guidance office. "This isn't the place to discuss consequences. The counselor is busy. I'm taking Andrew and we're going to his job interview. We can register tomorrow. Your tirades are only going to alienate Andrew and most certainly insure he does not go to summer school. As it is, he's left to get away from you." Andrew had left the office and was headed down the miles of hallway of the enormous school building. "Goodbye."

Later that day, Charity actually managed to get Andrew to agree to summer school, to call his father, "Thank him for letting you go to the interview; it will help the situation," and to talk his father into seeing the situation in a calmer light. Quite a day's work.

Andrew had at first tried to arrange some way to get out of summer school. "I don't need the course. I can get school level credit. I can take it next year; I can take it at college." School level credit for just one course meant no regents level diploma which meant three years of extremely hard studies were for naught. Unfair, Charity felt, but also unacceptable for Andrew to settle for want of one course, actually four credits.

"I don't care about Regents. And nobody outside of New York State does either." This was true, Charity knew. Her sister didn't even know what Regents were. "We have Regents exams, so we're still in school," Charity had told her over the phone. "What's that?" Chloe had asked.

"I just want to move out of the country or the state. I want to move to Hawaii."

Hawaii! That was Fieldlily's latest fantasy and just about on the seventeen year old level, Charity thought.

"That can be arranged!" Charity told Andrew. Near tearful hysteria before Charity had said this, Andrew now started to laugh.

It was a line Charity had learned from the Three Musketeers movie she had shown her seventh graders. The evil Cardinal Richelieu character had intoned it to Queen Anne when she said she'd rather die than sit next to him on the throne. "That can be arranged!" He shouted back at her.

Charity used the line and the intonation frequently to her kids after that. "I don't want to take this test. I'll take a zero. I'll go to detention. I'll leave and take an AWOL fine." "That can be arranged!" Charity would say, and it never failed to make them laugh and to defuse the situation.

So Andrew laughed and calmed down ("chilled" the kids called it) and began to consider serious alternatives. "You know, Mom, I really want to go to the reservation. I could go there and just be there and write."

This moved Charity. She knew she, and therefore Andrew, was part Cherokee, enough, she suspected, to enroll them as tribal members. She had felt an extreme urging to go searching for her lost Cherokee forebears, and now Andrew seemed to want it too. To Charity, it always felt like going home at last must feel. She promised Andrew that during the August vacation, they would go to the North Carolina Cherokee reservation. "Ok," Andrew agreed serenely and happily.

June 27

It was summer, high summer, the beginning of summer. It was hot, as hot and humid as it had been last weekend at the hotel. Charity went to bring Malcolm X, her huge Chow-Newfoundland mix dog, inside the basement on the stone tiles where it was cooler. He looked hot, even in the shade. Just as she unhooked his tie out chain, he spotted her cat, Sir Lancelot, coming around the side of the house and he took off, circling the cat, picking up speed while making a wide arc in the yard, gaining momentum as he ran up the driveway and down the street, like a dog on a mission. Charity knew where he was headed, where he always ran when he got away, down the street to Poochie, the neutered Golden Retriever. He'd charge right up to the door and jump half way up the screen in an effort to get to Poochie, his true love. Poochie would let out a howl from within but didn't jump, being fifteen years old, until his owner let him out and he and Malcolm would romp like puppies for hours.

But the last time Malcolm had gone running to Poochie, Poochie's owner had come out and told Malcolm and Charity that Pooch had to be put to sleep the day before, as he was dying of congestive heart failure. "That's what my father died of," Charity said, with some knowledge of what was involved. "Oh, I'm sorry," said Poochie's owner. "Don't be, it was six and a half years ago," Charity said. So Pooch wasn't there to run to anymore and Malcolm X skirted the house and ran to the woods by the river behind all the houses on Creek Locks Road.

He looked at her and Charity said "Come on, Malky," and he'd smirk and run on farther. They were behind a house and in an area Charity was unfamiliar with. This being a ninety-five degree day, and humid, Charity was covered with sweat. "Come to Mummy," she muttered, "Mummy will definitely spank," she thought. Malcolm ran on, into a little stream in the woods. Next to it where Charity found herself, was a sort of antique garbage dump with rusted springs and broken glass jutting up out of the poison ivy. "Come, Malcolm," she said sternly.

He ran on after a stray cat and treed it. Every time he barked the cat climbed higher. Charity hoped it knew how to get down. And she thought Malcolm was afraid of cats! He certainly was afraid of the ones she had at home!

When he finally headed out of the woods behind a house, the owners came out and Malcolm went right up to them. Total strangers! Go figure, she thought.

"Well, Eleanor, we have visitors," the man said. "I'm Dave," he said, "and you are...?" "Charity," she supplied, "and this is Malcolm, who's now in the doghouse." Going up to strangers without a glance at her, while making her chase him, drenched in sweat, bad doggie! She thought. "Shall I give him a drink?" Eleanor offered. "No, thanks," Charity said, "He drank out of the stream and we have to be going." "Nice meeting you," the all said to each other.

Charity reflected that this was the way she had met most of the neighbors in Creek Locks, walking or chasing her dog. Now everyone knew who Malcolm was by name and only knew her by sight when she was with him. It was just like when Andrew was little. He was social and outgoing even as a toddler, and everyone knew him and only knew her as "Andrew's mother." She didn't mind, but to be "Malcolm's mother" and Malcolm being a dog was a bit much.

Charity recalled the time in the Creek Locks Supermarket when Andrew was four, and a pretty, vaguely familiar-looking woman was ahead of them in line with a toddler in her shopping cart. She turned and said, "Hi, Andrew, did you get to ride on that swing?" As Charity belatedly recognized Jill Clayburgh, with a gasp, Ms. Clayburgh explained she had met Andrew and his father at the local playground when she was there with her daughter. "Yes, I did, Jill," Andrew replied. How was it that her four year old was on a comfortable first name basis with a famous actress? Charity wondered, stunned into speechlessness.

June 28

Charity sat out on her deck. All her pets, except the guinea pig, sat with her. It was June, it was not too hot, it was not hot at all, it was perfect. The trees surrounded the second story deck and the sky was a clear, true blue with a few brilliant white clouds for contrast. The fresh green of catalpa leaves added further contrast. It was a perfect moment. Charity never failed to sit out here but that she felt she was in a tree house, her own, adult, private tree house. It was on this very deck, six years ago, that she fully and completely mourned the passing of her father. Every one of her new pets had fallen off this deck once, like a sort of initiation, none of them had been hurt. On this deck she had written the first letter to her mother where she had ever permitted herself to say what she really felt. On that occasion, her mother had sent her a small loan that Charity had asked for, and, meanly and unfairly, Charity felt, had presented her with a bill for it plus the plane ticket her mother had given her to fly in to help after the birth of her sister's second child, which Charity had accepted, but not asked for. Charity quickly wrote a letter, returning the loan, and asking what her mother meant by adding on the plane ticket. Hadn't that been a gift? Hadn't Charity's presence the week after the birth, cooking, cleaning, and taking care of her preschool nephew, freed her mother of having to do that instead or to pay for a nurse? Hadn't that been her mother's idea? Charity suspected that it was her mother's new, rich and parsimonious husband who was behind the complaints and the mention of the debt. Nevertheless, she returned the check, torn in two, and for once voiced her real feelings about her mother's actions. Her mother called, then sent a letter saying she must not have made herself clear, she was sorry, of course she didn't mean to bring up the plane ticket, etc. She did not send a replacement loan check however. Smart woman, Charity had thought, because she would have definitely not accepted it then, small enough as it was. She never intended to ask for money from her mother again. She went around singing "God bless the child that's got its own," for a week after that.

It was a pity she didn't have the loan now, Charity thought. She could use it more than ever. She had gotten herself on a credit blacklist and couldn't seem to reestablish herself, even with her bank, which used to be local but had affiliated with a national banking institution which was cold and heartless about lending. Even if you'd had a loan before and repaid it in full, and Charity had had several, if you erred by even making late payments to any creditor, you were considered a bad credit risk, and were damned to debtor's hell for all eternity. Unfair! Charity moaned, to no avail. She desperately needed to replace her old Subaru. Fieldlily was whining for a computer with a modem. Get a job, she told him, sweetly, in so many words, I can't possibly do more than I already am.

She sat on the deck now, trying to figure out how on earth she could manage to overcome her debt and meet her financial obligations. Trying to rearrange her income into a budget that worked, trying to stabilize her spending and income. As she wrote, she sipped a very small glass of white wine. Fieldlily came out presently and sat next to her. He had been pleasant, for Fieldlily, these past few weeks, which he attributed to ingestion of colloidal minerals. "Drinking again? You're turning into quite the wino," he said, somewhat affectionately. Unmoved by the affection or the slur, Charity replied, "But darling, it makes you so much more tolerable." Charity immediately felt ashamed of herself and regretted what she said. It was, she realized, just the sort of blaming statement an alcoholic might have made. Fieldlily did not seem to mind. He went back inside for another dose of colloidal minerals.

June 29

Charity made a list of all the things she would do over her small vacation from the Academy.

She would have her coffee on the deck each beautiful morning.

She would weed her garden, fertilize it, get the lawn mower fixed, make a brick path.

She would update all the pets' shots and medical records.

She would clean out her closet and rearrange her bedroom.

She would reread her Alexander School notes and try to formulate a course on the subject.

She would get all her bills in order, the paperwork, if not the money.

She would make an appointment for a medical check-up.

She'd have her old medical records transferred.

She realized she hadn't been to a doctor herself for a decade. She sat out on the deck as she wrote her list. From high up in the old evergreen tree, two and a half times the height of the house, a dove cooed. A bee buzzed her head. "I'm not a flower, go away," she said and then laughed, because she was wearing a robe with pink roses on it.

From beyond the deck she could see her garden, carved out of the overgrown meadow that was her backyard, and beyond that the waist high weeds and the "pond" that was the overflow from the septic.

Mariah, her small female cat, begged to be let out by climbing the deck door screen. Charity went to do so.

June 30

Charity decided, studying her face in the mirror one morning, that it resembled nothing so much as a water color that had started to run.

Charity, being an English teacher and a writer, often supplied technical terms for one of her dance instructors, who was Russian. Over the years in class they had evolved it into an unspoken team effort. The instructor would demonstrate a move, and say, "This is called..." hesitating for only a moment, and Charity would call out the proper term - eleve, or arabesque, or spiral, the instructor would nod, satisfied, and Charity felt satisfied, as well.

Maybe I can't execute the move perfectly, but at least I can perfectly verbalize it. It was a mutually beneficial relationship, and the entire class gained by it.

July 1

Charity, the inveterate list-maker, made a list of things she would never do.

She would never live in a trailer, or own one.

She would never get rid of a pet she had already adopted.

She would never again own an American car.

She would never fail to recycle.

She would never remarry if she and Fieldlily did not work out.

She would always downshift.

If she promised to do something for the kids at the Academy, or for Andrew, she would never fail to do it, or she wouldn't promise.

If she ever conquered the clutter in her overstuffed house, she would never again let it go unchecked.

  Regarding the trailer, she had once remarked to a snobby friend of hers, who brought out the snob in Charity, that if she had played her cards right she could have been half way to owning her own trailer by then. It was a sarcastic and somewhat bitter comment, and her friend had loved it, and laughed haughtily.

She had kept what her vet called her original cats through several moves until they had both expired of natural causes at eighteen and nineteen years.

The only two cars she had bought herself were Subarus.

She had recycled since childhood, a trait engrained by her mother, for which Charity was grateful.

She had no intention of ever being involved with another man. She didn't even want to be involved with Fieldlily.

The brakes on her old red Subaru only had to be replaced at 170,000 miles so zealous a downshifter was Charity. She taught Andrew to downshift as well.

She never made promises to the kids or anyone else unless she knew she was able to keep them. Period.

She had once, before Fieldlily entered her life, managed to neatly organize her house. She had recently begun a campaign to conquer the paper clutter, with plans to move on to the closets, and with Andrew's help, the cellar.

God willing, she'd even get to the garage. She decided for the closets and cellar she needed the help of organizational items such as cedar blocks, shelving and garment units, and anti-moth and anti-mold products.

Charity decided she was a committed, organized and praiseworthy person after analyzing her latest list and she realized this with more than a trace of surprise and with no hubris at all. Wasn't commitment a type of promise and didn't keeping one's promises entail a certain amount of charity; of giving of oneself? True to my name, after all, Charity thought.

July 2

Charity was sick of students who couldn't spell the most basic words, word for world, or in for and or who for how (how? She wondered,) who cursed at her when she asked them to take out their notebooks, who spoke in graphic detail during homeroom about their exploits of torturing and killing animals.

July 3

Her former husband was a liar. Could he truly be as forgetful of his past rages as he claimed he was? Could he himself honestly say he never ranted or lied? How convenient his memory was. Could people who didn't remember what they did claim innocence for their actions?

July 4

She just couldn't do it. She couldn't. She just couldn't, Charity thought. She couldn't teach summer school, exhort Andrew to get up early everyday, try to arrange finances, or rearrange income, to meet all her expenses, especially trying to buy another car and put Andrew on the insurance policy. She wasn't eligible for any loans except usurious ones with 25% interest rates "for good people with bad credit" and even if she did take out one of those, assuming she could get it, she'd have a heck of a time trying to pay it back on the Academy salary, even with her extra income from the hotel and other massage therapy work.

She was sick of the Academy - she needed a respite! The ten days off before summer session weren't nearly enough and, as usual, there was no extra money for a brief vacation or even a meal out at a restaurant! Plus, several days were put in at the hotel, the money always being needed. Summer Session was brutal anyway and even teaching over the summer, her salary was way below public school teachers, by about 25% coincidentally.

Oh she'd been through this so many times in her mind! She was sick of it. She tried to be positive, she tried to be thankful that she had a job at all, that she was able to work with kids who really needed her help, even if they didn't want it! That she had the vacation time she had... It was no use. If this wasn't burnout, to use an outmoded term, she didn't know what was. Even in other years, she had managed to go visit her family or to the Alexander workshop in Vermont that she loved, it was a refresher in all ways. Not this year! The financial pressures were mounting and Fieldlily was clamoring to be set up in business, but expected her, as usual, to advance the money and he, as usual, would not raise a finger to bring in anything, because of his fragility, his exquisite spirituality that mustn't be tarnished, his superiority to any job he, as a basically unschooled and unskilled person, would be likely to get.

If he wasn't an example to Andrew to stay in school and to finish college, she didn't know who was! She did feel slightly guilty when she thought these things because even without formal education or certificates, Fieldlily was self-taught and capable of deep thinking and solid solutions. She also encouraged him to get away from low-paying, degrading positions, which didn't make much of a difference to their income, but raised their taxes noticeably. So she had no one to blame but herself, really, for her situation. She could look for a public school job herself and enjoy more pay and summers off. She could encourage Fieldlily to work at some mild job for a short while until he launched his business. If she did neither, who was to blame for her situation but herself?

Was supporting Fieldlily and working at the Academy becoming a thorn in her side, causing festering resentment all around? If so, then she was far from the selfless being who gave of herself for divinely ordained reasons that she supposed herself to be.

She thought about this out on her deck on the Fourth of July, as she resisted planning for summer classes, as she tried not to think of working in a hot, windowless room at the hotel all day tomorrow, as she tried not to panic about the mounting bills. Damn! She wished she'd gone to the library yesterday and taken out some good books by women authors, like Alice Walker or Maya Angelou or Julie Hecht.

July 7

"So, what were you in a past life?" Jason asked Charity.

She was driving him to pick up some last minute items before he left for Long Island to stay with his birth mother (his term). He had been with her and Fieldlily for a month and things had been tense. The house was just too small for that much problematic interaction. Charity had been worried about it from the start, when she remembered Jason's two month stay with them last winter. Then Fieldlily had been adamant that Jason must go, and Jason had moved to a hotel where he'd lived before. Then he'd lost one job after another, gotten deep into a depression and climbed out of it just enough to attempt suicide, call them again, and it was Fieldlily and Charity to the rescue and more of the same problems from last winter: lack of money, an extra mouth to feed, arguments between Fieldlily and Jason, Charity trying to remain calm and reasonable, but angered when the hot water was left on, running up the electric bill, or water was left running when Jason was washing dishes, this after his shower, and after doing two loads of laundry, filling up the septic tank, causing it to overflow; or things got broken carelessly, or thrown out instead of recycled, and to remind Jason of any or all of these things made her feel like she was policing him or that she had a pre-adolescent child or a puppy to housebreak.

"Damned if I know," she answered.

July 9

Charity sat in her hot classroom with her hot, disgruntled students. It was only second period. There were two more to go before lunch. Then there were two periods (even hotter, the sun beating in full force by that time of day) and an open period, plus today she had detention. Damn!

She had given her students a small writing assignment: write five sentences beginning "I remember". She then had them choose one to use as a topic sentence for a paragraph titled I remember. A lot of the students wrote about injuries involving stitches or broken bones. Others wrote about being sent to the Academy. Two of the newer boys wrote about being shot. One still had a bullet lodged in his shoulder. One wrote about running drugs. He was twelve at the most.

July 13

Charity looked at the newest students. They seemed, for the most part, to be thugs. It was going to be a tough year. She wondered if she had it in her. Help, she silently prayed.

That weekend, Charity worked at the hotel for one afternoon. It was gorgeous weather, but Fieldlily was showing signs of restlessness, boredom and lethargy, so she wasn't all that unhappy to go to work. Besides, she needed the money. Checks were bouncing, and Academy payday was not until the coming week.

She carried her own water to the hotel. She had read the town where it was located was suffering from a giardia contamination throughout their water supply. She was pretty sure the hotel had its own water supply, but she wasn't taking any chances. She knew about giardia, an insidious intestinal parasite that required an unbelievably strong medication to kill it. Charity had been at the hotel three weeks earlier, when the outbreak had first been detected. It was horribly hot and humid that day and she had drunk freely from the water cooler. Now she hoped it was hotel water and not town water. The article she read said it took ten days to two weeks to show symptoms. She hoped after three weeks she was beyond worry. Usually it took things more than the specified time to show up in her, but she figured after three weeks she should be sure.

She had to laugh at the irony. Marney always carried her own water anyway, not trusting hotel water and being of a paranoid frame of mind about everything. Now she was justified. It was sickeningly funny how paranoid personalities, like Marney and Fieldlily, only needed one instance for justification, like the water incident at the hotel, to feel that all of their paranoid fantasies were true and worthy of holding onto.

July 14

Charity and Fieldlily had a fight. It was the first in a long time. Charity had mentioned a twenty year old memory of an American Indian friend of hers and a photograph she had taken where he was at a park in Queens, staring at a single fenced in buffalo. The two solemnly contemplated one another, the caged buffalo, the city-bound Indian, both alone. Charity had been friends with him, felt an affinity. They were both Virgos, both born in the same year, both of Indian ancestry (he was pure blooded, 100% though) both grew up in cities, away from their heritage and not on a reservation. She wondered what happened to him, where he was. She wondered if he ever thought about her.

"Isn't he the one who flirted a lot with you?" Fieldlily had asked. Charity, confused by the fact that she was having a feeling memory and that Fieldlily was intruding with something quite different, disregarding the feeling she was having, said no.

Fieldlily blew up. "That's not what you told me before! You're always lying!"

Charity was really hurt. She had already been hurt earlier that day when she hinted she was feeling sexual toward him and he had said that he couldn't be intimate with her until they resolved their communication problems.

Charity had felt immediately rejected. She felt undesirable and unattractive. She wished Fieldlily wouldn't bring up flirting when she was having deep feelings about something and trying to work them through. She wished he would realize that she felt unattractive and when she felt unattractive, she didn't feel like flirting with anyone, or even talking about flirting, especially about a twenty plus years ago flirtation. Especially when she was feeling a deeper emotion. Especially when that was Fieldlily's complaint, that she didn't feel her feelings, that she couldn't communicate, that she wouldn't be able to communicate until she felt her feelings.

July 18

Charity hated summer school teaching. By 10:00 it was a steam bath in her room. Construction sent dust and diesel fumes into the air when the windows were open. When they were closed, it was stifling even with two fans going. The kids kept turning the fans on themselves, switching off the button that allowed it to circulate air. Charity kept telling them not to, imposing school fines on them. It did no good. Either way, fines or not, fans or not, it was unbearable.

Afternoons were the worst. The assistant education director, a chirpy, foolish little woman, had wanted teachers to volunteer to do 4-H club projects with the kids for a county fair display. No one volunteered, so Ms. Chirp had decreed that the afternoon elective courses (a misnomer, since no one, kids or staff, had "elected" those classes) would be the 4-H clubs. Charity, with a room full of hot city kids, most of whom didn't even want to take a walk around the Academy campus, (the bees! The Mosquitoes! The killer squirrels! Such dangers! Poison ivy!) refused to participate. She was not interested in 4-H, or she would have volunteered. She was an English teacher, trying to interest the kids in writing skills. This was not 4-H material. Whose idea was this anyway?

Charity felt burnt out, exhausted. She needed time off. She needed a real vacation. She needed to go swimming when it was this hot. None of these seemed like a possibility.

July 20

Charity felt discouraged once again. Life revolved itself around working, either at the Academy or at the hotel, paying bills, bouncing checks, paying the fees for the bounced checks, fending off creditors, trying not to worry but to trust in God's infinite supply which seemed lacking to her, but maybe that was her lack of faith? dealing with anxiety about Andrew's future, (which he didn't seem the least bit anxious about,) Fieldlily's irritations and wants, Andrew's father's irrational anger and vindictiveness, longing for a vacation, for things to be different (better!) for there to be enough, there never seemed to be enough. Not enough money, not enough time off, not enough respite from worry, not enough affection.

She knew things weren't even bad. She wasn't suffering from some fatal or dreaded disease, and neither was Andrew or Fieldlily, for all his hypochondria and paranoia and running to doctors to be checked out and tested (expensively, and not always covered by insurance, another bill to worry over.) She had a job, or rather, jobs. Andrew seemed to be headed in the right direction. So she didn't have major troubles the way she might, the way others she knew did. She just had garden variety troubles and those were weighing her down. She didn't know where to turn. Her life seemed so dreary and destined to remain so, without improvement and with very little else.

July 21

When Charity was seriously troubled, worried or depressed, she did one of two things: listened to the Requiems of Mozart and/or Verdi, with the bass turned up, or read the poetry of Sylvia Plath. When she was particularly angry at Fieldlily, she read either of two short stories by Shirley Jackson about wives murdering their husbands. Once she had read one aloud to Fieldlily, chuckling, and once or twice guffawing out loud, there was no other word for it. He didn't quite appreciate the humor.

Then she would write about her current crisis in her journal, which was rapidly turning into a complaint book, listing her gripes, concerns and despairs. What she wanted it to be was a witty observation of life in general and a study in depth of hers in particular, which was definitely not the case recently.

Now, upset by financial burdens, and her somewhat loveless (and sexless, let's be frank) marriage, she listened to Mozart's requiem and contemplated her life's work.

She wondered if she was answering her true calling, would she then have enough money? The "do what you love, the money will follow," school of thought. She wanted to believe this but had her doubts. She wondered if she tithed more regularly, truly gave 10% of her income, if this would miraculously tip the monetary scales in her favor. Again, she wanted to believe, but did not, whole heartedly. The "Sanctus" began. Perhaps it was because she felt if she gave ten percent of her inadequate income at this point, she would be further in the hole. She already figured her expenses exceeded her income by more than 10%. Besides her last check to an organization had bounced. Still, she tried to give when and where she could. "Sanctus." Her problem, she decided, was she was not doing what she loved or what she had always wanted to do. Which was what? She honestly didn't know. When she was young, her two ambitions had been to be a writer or a ballet dancer, of which she was neither. Far below that on the list was being a teacher but mostly because she loved school.

Ballet lessons ended at age eleven, much to her dismay, hence she lacked the training to be a ballet dancer. About the same time, she began keeping a diary and she had always written her own stories and enjoyed school writing assignments, which for her were easy. Not so for everyone! Once her friend Pam, who did not find writing easy at all, begged for her help on an assignment to write a story about a picture of pioneer life in Ohio, their state. Charity had agreed, somewhat reluctantly, because she didn't want to cheat and this felt a bit like cheating on Pam's part, if not hers. So she had written her story and then, disguising her writing to look like Pam's, she had written another story in what she felt would be Pam's style. What happened next galled her. The teacher, Mrs. Davis, had chosen Pam's story for display, commenting on how good it was. Hey, Charity wanted to shout, that's my story up there on the bulletin board! Her own was not, of course, chosen this time.

Charity Begins at Home   119

Thinking this over, she considered if being a ghost writer might have been her calling?

The Kyrie began. Her favorite section. She had not, after all, become an author. (Kyrie! Reis!) She had a half-written novel, On the Way Home, about a young middle-aged woman somewhat like herself who was trying to find her place in life before it was over (her life, not the novel) but her agonies seemed to be adolescent or early twenties at most; by middle age, shouldn't one know? She had a stack of maybe fifty poems, enough for a book, but not all of them book quality. She had a novelette if such a thing existed anymore in 1997, about the memoirs of her old cat, Rachel written in the first person in Rachel's voice. None of these was published or even polished. So she was not an author, not yet.

Nor was she a musician, although she had begun piano lessons at seven and continued for eleven years. When she was ten she had learned to play clarinet and later, oboe which she continued through high school. While she loved her piano teacher, and respected the music teachers in school, she dropped the study of music altogether in college, not unhappily. She had wanted to study dance all those years, not music, anyway. The one thing on which she confronted her mother early in adulthood was why. Why had she been made to study music all that time and drop dance?

Her mother answered at once, "I thought you'd be a teacher and you would need piano. We couldn't afford both piano and ballet lessons." Charity had taken some satisfaction in pointing out that she hadn't become an elementary school teacher and besides, they now hired music teachers in addition to classroom teachers, so even if she had become an elementary teacher she wouldn't need to know how to play the piano. Not that she was sorry she had learned, she just wanted to dance. So she had taken ballet as an elective in college and had studied it in graduate school, going on after that to study modern dance, her current passion. She had even taught movement and dance classes for a while to children. So much for piano!

"Agnus Dei," sang the tape player. Besides, why extra money for oboe lessons, but not ballet? "Agnus Dei!"

Just what was her ambition? Charity worried if she had any ambition at all that was her own. Being a teacher was her mother's choice, clearly, although Charity had resisted that one until she was in graduate school, preferring to major in English and Philosophy in undergraduate school. At that point, she had overheard a friend say that she planned to go to graduate school and then teach on the college level. Charity had tried that on and decided as a profession it fit her too. So she elected to go to graduate school and most of the way through her masters in English had suddenly decided she wanted to help humanity by teaching mentally retarded or learning disabled children. So she reapplied for admission to the masters program in Education, had trained to teach Special Education and hadn't gotten a single job doing that since. Instead, she ended up with deviant teenagers and had taught them more or less continually ever since.

She was still doing this at the Academy, but less and less happily.

So what was her ambition, her calling, her life's work? Too late to dance - too old - should she try to publish her writing? She couldn't live off that, of course, but with supplements from doing massage at the hotel, plus teaching private Alexander Technique lessons?

Or what?

Did she have any desires that were truly her own?

It was the answer to this question that genuinely troubled her.

July 28

Mid Summer (school) and, after a brief hiatus from hot weather, it was back. Charity longed for a real vacation: a week (or two) at Cape Cod, a study week in Vermont, those lush mountains, with her Alexander colleagues, a weekend by a lake somewhere.

Instead, what she did was take a vacation from worrying about bills, and from debting. She located a book she had bought, oh, say, four years ago, on getting out of debt permanently. She began to follow the steps to the "back in the black" program.

Things began to happen almost at once.

A student loan for Andrew came through, which turned out to be unnecessary, as his grandfather agreed to pay for his tuition. The interest free loan could be paid back, a little at a time, through payroll deduction. The money could be used to replace her old car.

She felt lighter and happier than she had in years.

Fieldlily announced his determination to once again resume his consulting practice, implying he would once again be bringing in an income.

Charity Begins at Home 123

Andrew got a summer job, and then a better one, relieving her of having to give him an allowance, lunch money, or even rides or gas money for his friends. He was relieved and happy to be going off to college in the Fall, instead of back to the high school where he felt increasingly unsafe.

The friend who had borrowed her sewing machine and moved, moved back and returned it. She could now sew some of the clothes she had been mentally designing and it wouldn't cost her a cent, plus she'd feel she had some creative outlet.

The book suggested investing in a work-sponsored retirement account and promised many returns from this, monetary and other. She took the initial steps and couldn't wait for the results, she was so certain that this system worked. And because she was so sure, the efforts she put in were sincere and forceful, insuring many happy returns.

July 29

Charity's "vacation" was short-lived, more short-lived than the two day break she took from summer school teaching.

The loan for Andrew's schooling was approved - for one quarter of the suggested amount. Not even enough for one semester. And not enough time to raise the difference, since she had put on the application it was needed on or before the first which was Friday and the inadequate money wasn't coming through until then.

It wasn't necessary in Andrew's case, but what if it had been? What if this was the only way to afford school and it wasn't enough? There wasn't even enough time to seek other avenues of assistance. What did they mean, it was to enable kids to go to college? It wouldn't even help if he needed tuition by a certain date and he didn't have it. He wouldn't even be able to go! It was an insult, a slap in the face, an outrage to have so little approved, so late in the day.

Not that he needed it. He didn't, he was lucky, she was lucky. But... oh damn, damn, damn, she needed the money! No replaced car. No easing of worries. Well the no-debt financial program she had placed herself on specified: no more debt. That was certainly being driven home. She couldn't even go into debt now if she wanted to. No debt today.

She felt like crying. She felt like sobbing. Well, Fieldlily would just have to let her drive the car she was paying for. It wasn't like he had anywhere he had to be everyday, like she did. They could do with one car better than most. Why should the car sit in the driveway, day after day, on the off-chance that Fieldlily needed to go two miles down the road for cigarettes? When he needed it, for therapy, or longer trips, she could make arrangements for a ride to work, or he could take her. She didn't need to inconvenience people everyday, so Fieldlily could have the car constantly at his disposal. What was she thinking? She didn't need to be inconvenienced everyday! Let him be carless more often than not! She was the one paying for it; she was the one with the jobs; she was the one to do the odious tasks, like shopping and banking and post office runs, she needed to have a car at her disposal more than he did!

That day she dressed in black, to match her black mood.

July 30

She was not often at home mid-day, mid-week, mid-summer, but she was today. And, except for the pets, she was alone. It was hot but not humid, a perfectly clear sky above, shady on the half of the deck where she sat. High summer, and she was at leisure! For the moment, she was not worried about money, the house in need of a thorough cleaning, Andrew's future, or the health of anyone; herself, Fieldlily, her pets, her mother, her friends. Instead, Charity sat listening to the harmonious cacophony of bird and bee song, neighborhood dogs barking, occasional motors from far off lawn mowers. A plane buzzed lazily overhead; a hummingbird buzzed her ear; the play of light on the drive comforted and elated her somehow. The phone did not ring. Charity was at peace. Wasn't this the most anyone could ask of a vacation?

July 31

Charity assigned her students to write five sentences about five things they missed. She wrote the assignment along with them, as she usually did. She wrote;

1. I miss going to Cape Cod with my ex-in-laws.
2. I miss going out to dinner with my parents.
3. I miss having enough money.
4. I miss MYF (Methodist Youth Fellowship.)
5. I miss... just what did she miss? Not so many big things, and yet so many little things, like being able to call her father anytime (he had died six and a half years ago) or going to foreign films at a town across the river. (Fieldlily refused to go to movies, or films, or most places. He was actually phobic, but covered it by saying everyone else, and the activities they chose, were "neurotic."

She missed the feelings of stimulation, excitement and, oddly, security of her undergraduate years; the intellectual blooming and recognition, the freedom, the passionate protests against political repression and right wing-ism, the protests against "The War," the Viet Nam war, that was.

She missed the large, old, gracious house she grew up in. She missed summers past, swimming in pools or at the ocean, smelling Coppertone, hearing bees buzz, seeing lightning bugs, getting browner, with freckles across her nose, feeling sun on her face and shoulders, enjoying long, long days, and months and months of leisure.

August 5

Not often, but sometimes, Charity would wake up in the middle of the night, at 2 or 3 or 4:00, and be unable to get back to sleep. At these times, she would not fight to go back to sleep, but instead would let her mind wonder over a number of disjointed topics. On this night, she wondered;

If she would rather be lying next to someone other than Fieldlily, or if she'd prefer to be lying here alone. If the new Pekingese puppy, Maggie, who woke her up in the first place, was the reason Mariah, her female cat, was acting strangely. Or was she acting the way Anya, her sister, had acted just before she died of feline leukemia? Charity hoped, prayed, that Mariah wasn't sick, or if so, that she'd pull through. She lay awake and worried about that one for a while. Charity was passionately attached to her cats.

She thought about replacing her old car, which would mean going into debt, if she dared risk it.

She wondered if she should look for a more lucrative job. She wished she could work at home. Tonight, she mostly wondered about the Sheppard murder case.

She had recently gotten a book out of the library that she had waited weeks for about the Sheppard murder. She felt almost personally involved in the case, having grown up in Ohio during the time of the murder, the appeals, the trails, the incessant stories in the paper, on the news. She couldn't, she realized, have remembered the actual murder. She would only have been three at the time. She vividly remembered the infamous bad press Dr. Sam Sheppard had gotten. She remembered hearing the word doctor and, of course, associating doctor with her own father. She could no more imagine her own father killing her mother or anyone else, than she could imagine the sun coming up in the West. Therefore, she couldn't conceive of a doctor murdering someone. As he had said, he was committed to preserving life, not taking it. Something must be terribly wrong, somewhere.

This was her childhood and early adolescence, when she was taught, and believed, that newspapers only printed factual information that could be verified. This was before the bloody civil rights demonstrations and the bloodier still Viet Nam War, and before Charity lost her innocence and learned that yes, indeed, innocent people were made to suffer by the news media, which often did not relate the truth, just opinions of someone. Of course, then it wasn't the "news media," it was just "the press."

Charity remembered actually meeting Sam Sheppard once, briefly. Her friend Stephanie and she had stopped by Stephanie's father's office building the summer of 1969, the year they graduated from high school. Stephanie's father, Mr. Brown, (as opposed to Charity's father, Dr. Brown) owned the building, so Stephanie knew he had rented an office to the infamous Dr. Sam Sheppard. His office door was open, and he was on the phone, and when he hung up,

Charity Begins at Home 131

they were introduced. Charity felt a chill. At that time, many people were still convinced he was a wife murderer. Was he, Charity wondered? He didn't seem like one, he just seemed like a normal person who appeared to have suffered a lot. He was only 45 or 46. He looked sad and beaten. Charity figured they didn't let convicted murders out on parole, so he must be cleared. This was on the eve of her innocence being shattered. Besides, he was a celebrity. The first celebrity she had ever met face to face. She felt thrilled. He died soon after that.

Looking back from her vantage point of 45 years to the time she had been Andrew's age, Charity felt more keenly what the man's personal pain must have been, and she realized, from the viewpoint of a parent who also worked with troubled, abandoned, neglected and sometimes orphaned kids, how damaging and dreadful it must have been for Dr. Sheppard's child, who was only seven. Charity's heart went out to that seven year old boy, losing his mother to death, and in essence, his father to the so-called justice system. Why did the press not realize what their poisonous statements were doing to a completely blameless, traumatized boy?

August 10

Charity had had a bad few days.

With the introduction of a Pekingese puppy, which Fieldlily had insisted he wanted, then said no, he didn't really mean it, one of her cats went AWOL, then finally came back but was acting sick or strange. Charity was worried that the stress of a new strange animal in the house had activated her feline leukemia virus, making her vulnerable to any number of illnesses. The puppy woke her up at night, naturally, so naturally, Fieldlily, a notoriously poor sleeper, woke up and just as naturally for him, became disturbed, angry, irrational; blaming Charity for his inability to sleep, his illnesses, which he said resulted from the stress this caused, and basically all the stress in his life became her fault.

Charity snapped, said something, she forgot what, and Fieldlily erupted, shouting that she was demented, neurotic, and totally unaware of hearing what she sounded like.

Charity broke down, sobbing, and cried and cried and cried. Finally she told him she wished she could die, she felt that worthless, her own father had said, probably more than once, that she had been a pain "since she was born, crying all the time," and she knew then that she couldn't get it right, right from birth, hadn't her own father said so? After a long pause, Fieldlily commented, "That's a messed up thing to say!"

Messed up, indeed.

August 14

Charity waited in front of her house, futilely, she was beginning to think, for a ride to a dance workshop for which she had registered. Fieldlily had taken the one working car to the dentist. It had been a half hour, and no ride had shown up. As it took twenty-five minutes to get to the dance studio, and she had asked a young dancer who lived in the same town to give her a ride, given her instructions to get to her house, and they had agreed to leave by 9:00, Charity could only conclude she had been forgotten. It seemed to be the theme of her life for the moment.

Last week, the day after the Big Fight with Fieldlily, Charity had seen her therapist and broken down into what, for her, was hysterics.

"We fight all the time. He always tells me how reprehensible and wrong I am. And I must be worthless! (She was becoming tearful now, the hysterics breaking through) no one ever remembers me, or my name, or what I do, or credits me with having any skill or knowledge or talent! (More tears). And I can't even support myself or anyone else, like my son! I can't get a loan for anything, and I'm losing ground monthly financially, no matter how

Charity Begins at Home

hard I work! I'm just no good at anything, useless, no good at all."

9:40. Class began at 9:30. She had definitely been forgotten. Again.

August 18

So she hadn't attended the one class and when she went back the next day, the instructor said, "Missed you yesterday!" and he had added her name. So much for being forgettable. She persevered, in spite of the fact that she felt ungainly, foolish, stiff and aged. "My leotard is older than most of the people in this room," she thought. It was true. The particular garment dated from her college days. If most of the company's dancers were in their twenties, it wasn't even an exaggeration. In one week, Charity would be 46.

She had trouble remembering the sequences of steps; she didn't know why. Was it lack of skill, unfamiliarity, past injuries, or could it be the clinically diagnosed but never confirmed Lyme disease?

She began to think of the weekday two hour class as her daily dose of humility, if not humiliation. She tried not to let it bother her when she stumbled and forgot the sequence. She tried to work from where she was and not to compare when her leg was not as high as her neighbor's at the barre. She tried to be humble and invisible. She tried to keep her tears in until she was home and in private. She tried to just let herself be, to enjoy the moment, to allow her feelings to be there. And they were. For some reason this type of movement (or maybe this moment in her life?) was bringing up a lot of emotion. If only, she thought, I could translate it into exquisite movement or self respect.

August 21

Mostly what it brought up was sadness. She felt sorry for herself (what else was new?) she felt overwhelmed by her life. She had gotten over feeling like she couldn't do anything right - now she felt like she couldn't do anything at all! The image in the bathroom mirror of a morning repulsed her. The image in the dance studio mirror sickened her, when she dared to look at all. I look worse moving than I look standing still, and that's pretty awful, she thought. She was vaguely aware of something else, though. Underneath it all, she knew that this preoccupation with her appearance was really a form of avoidance. She was avoiding confronting the root, the basis, of her feelings of inadequacy, unease, inferiority. She wasn't willing to deal with the underlying trauma she knew was there. But it was there, waiting to trip her up at every turn, and it would continue to do so until she faced it head on. When she acknowledged this, she didn't worry about the image in the mirror. So what if I look older? I am older - I have a son starting college. I'm not twenty anymore, I'm the mother of someone approaching twenty. It's the truth, undeniable and unavoidable. And I don't want to deny or avoid it. That would be to deny Andrew's existence, and I certainly wouldn't do that, not even if I could!

She felt like she was getting somewhere with this line of reasoning. She couldn't wait to tell her therapist, who had been right to insist she take this workshop, feeling it would shift something for her. It had, and would surely continue to do so.

August 22

But what was it shifting? All she felt, all she seemed to attract, was dissatisfaction. The dance workshop was making her feel inadequate, unnoticed and unappreciated. No one was interested in her, in what she did, who she was.

Even her oral tastes were going unsatisfied. It had turned cool, so she went to buy some red wine for her nightcap. She had very little money to spend, so she opted for a burgundy over a cabernet, and it was the wrong choice. It was an American burgundy, New York State, in fact, and it was terrible. Not terrible enough to return, like it had gone bad or something, just not good. Money wasted, taste for red wine unsated.

The next day, after budgeting for the weekend, she took a few dollars and stopped by an ice cream parlor near her bank for a chocolate malted, which she had been craving. The owner said she was out of malted, could it be just chocolate? And Charity had said fine. It wasn't. It tasted like they forgot the chocolate, too, and it didn't even have much flavor if it was vanilla ice cream. It was flat, nearly flavorless, with a hint of chocolate, which was worse than no chocolate, it was such a tease for what she really wanted.

Orally unsatisfied... so even little treats were proving major disappointments. Maybe little treats weren't what she was seeking, and that's why they were so unable to satisfy her longings. Her mother used to say, "You're not hungry, you're bored." Not bored, maybe, but not physically hungry, either. Looking for something to go right, to feel right, to be different than her depressing, oppressive existence.

August 25

Well, it was here, her 46 birthday. She went to her daily workshop (it was paid for, after all) and, as usual, felt near tears at points during the class. When one of her regular dance instructors, who was taking the class too, complained at the combination's start, "This is so disorganized! They don't know what they're doing! It's so loose, I mean, I know this is the country, but really...!" Charity suddenly felt relieved. She was so caught up in feeling bad, she couldn't see beyond it to analyze what might be contributing to it.

Nevertheless, she slipped out early. No sense in ruining a perfectly good birthday by too much humility. She stopped at the gas station/convenient store, because the car read empty and when she left, she held open the door for the person behind her, as was her custom. When she looked to see who it was, she recognized one of the street people from the town. As she made eye contact, he fervently thanked her and said, "Have a good day!" She felt lifted up by this, and suddenly the bible verse about entertaining angels unaware popped into her head. For someone who has little use for organized Christianity, I certainly quote the bible a lot, she thought, if only to myself. But the man's joy in being seen and acknowledged made her wonder how often it happened to him. It had been a mutually beneficial encounter, it was only seconds long, it cost nothing, and it meant a great deal to both of them.

She went home, Andrew was up, and announced his intention to stay home all day and to do anything around the house for her birthday. She asked him to clean his room. He also had picked flowers for her from his father's house.

Fieldlily had actually bought her a card and written a note of gratitude for her support and admiration for her energy.

Her mother sent her usual check. Her sister had called last night. Charity used part of the check to take Andrew, Fieldlily and herself out to dinner.

Then, because she had overheard Andrew on the phone saying he didn't know if he could go out anywhere, "cause it's my mom's birthday," she told him that she really had wanted the three of them to go out to dinner, but she didn't expect him to stay in all evening, too.

Best of all, she hadn't reminded anyone that her birthday was coming up, and they had remembered, anyway.

And, in spite of the weather predictions for "mostly cloudy, 40% chance of rain," the sun had shown all day, and it was blessedly warm, not too hot.

September 6

It had been the strangest week, Charity reflected. The spectacularly tragic death of Princess Diana, the quiet, beatific death of Mother Teresa a week later, and the start of a new term at the Academy sandwiched in between. Not to mention Andrew's start at community college instead of his last year at City High School. So many changes. Such endings and beginnings.

She felt the deaths of both Princess Diana and Mother Teresa keenly, obviously for different reasons, and shed tears on hearing of them, both times. Diana, a fellow divorced mother, and believer in helping those in your power to help, and Mother Teresa, a saint, to Charity, whose selfless devotion to charity for her entire life had lead Charity, at one time, to seriously consider joining her order. They both represented the ultimate in charitable works to Charity, they both spoke to her philosophy of doing good where you are able, with whatever resources and skills were available to you.

So she lost two of her role models and inspirations in one week. She had mentioned how sad she found it one day at work and Anne, her co-worker, had commented, "Princess Di, I can see, she was young, but Mother Teresa was old, why find that sad?" How could Charity express that, yes, she was old, but that her passing was like a light going out for all of them?

Not long before, she had said goodbye to two long-held dreams: the first was to be a dancer (another link to Princess Diana.) With the end of the intensive dance workshop, where Charity had felt so out of place and clumsy, she had to let go of the dream she secretly held of being "discovered" and invited to join a dance company. If the professional company members whose class she endured were too polite to look at her askance, they certainly were not impressed with her talent and ability, either. Charity became philosophical about it, in the end. "If I were meant to be a dancer, it would certainly have happened before now. It's not in my life plan, that's all."

This was especially bourne out by the circumstance that she never even got to see the culminating performances of the company. Both evening performances were sold out - not even standing room - and she couldn't see the last minute matinee, because she had to work at the hotel and couldn't turn down the lucrative holiday weekend pay.

She had actually convinced Fieldlily to drive with her the last night of the performance to see if perhaps some reservations or "comp" tickets hadn't been claimed, to no avail. The house manager was very apologetic, but explained that it was so overcrowded, even the theater staff had nowhere to view the performances. So Charity left, disappointed. Fieldlily, seeing her disappointment, offered to go wherever she wanted instead, but then complained so stridently about how bad he was feeling (my allergies! My back! The house dust and mold! Our mattress!) that Charity felt she wouldn't dare insist on going somewhere else. She even, in a rare stand, told him so. "Why would I insist on going somewhere, when you don't feel well and obviously just want to go home? It's not in my nature to be so self-involved, disappointed or not!" It was said strongly, clearly, and without bitterness. Fieldlily heard, and understood.

And the next morning, Charity saw the headlines about Princess Diana, who had wanted to be a dancer and didn't, just like Charity.

The second dream was about having her own family - being the mother of several children, with a stable, supportive man as their father. With Andrew's imminent departure for college, Charity had to let go of any such notion. "Andrew is my only child, and our relationship is the only family I am going to have." Fieldlily's only daughter lived with her mother, and even though it was only one town away, they rarely saw her. Charity felt she had never developed a relationship with her and probably never would, although she was a lovely girl and Charity would have liked to.

She realized that it was also too late to develop family traditions and to influence Andrew's spiritual growth much. She hoped that what she had consciously managed to do as he was growing up would be sufficient. She hoped her own personal struggles and travails at the same time period didn't cause her to be unconscious of what Andrew's needs were, or to harm him in any way.

He seemed to be ok, with the exception of a poor relationship recently with his father, which of course his father blamed her for, and of course anyone outside the situation could see was mostly self-induced by the father's undeveloped maturity. Also the fact that Andrew wanted to be mostly with his peers at any given time, but that was pretty normal for any 17 year old.

Well, I tried to do the best I could, within my knowledge and abilities and limits of what I could do and thought best, she concluded. It's part of my soul growth, and Andrew's too, and who is to say it's not part of some divine plan, just the way things unfolded?

The first week at the Academy was wearing, as was to be expected. Charity felt tired, since she wasn't used to getting up quite so early. The construction was going full force with all the noise and dust that created. Classrooms were temporarily moved around, and had to be gotten in order. New kids had arrived, to be introduced and slowly evaluated. And new "standards" were being initiated. This fascinated Charity, who had taught for some years, and always held herself and her students to a much higher standard than the school's somewhat lax administrators ever did.

Well, let them suggest higher general standards, she had probably already met them. When the Academy announced that a departing teacher, with less qualifications or experience than most of the Academy staff, would be a "consultant" for the first two weeks, and would be instructing the teachers as to their lesson plans, Charity felt miffed. Why would they assume someone with less training or experience should be placed in a superior position. With the same continuing education as they all got, why would this person know any more than the rest about upgrading lesson plans?

This was the same officious little person whom Charity had overheard saying that she assumed a student who had misbehaved by spitting on a construction worker from the window had been in Charity's classroom when it happened. He wasn't.

So this little chirp is going to come in and tell me how to run my classroom and how to write a lesson plan? Charity fumed. This would be a major test of her constraint and circumspection. We'll see, Charity thought. We'll see.

And then, the school counselor whose degree was in sociology, not education or psychology, had the gall to ask if she might offer her observations and suggestions for improving what Charity did in her classroom.

So much for the much-vaunted "professional autonomy" offered by the Academy, in lieu of an actual professional salary.

With all these upgradings and interferences, with the summer program, with the low pay (even if you worked the loathsome summer program) Charity concluded she would be better off doing something else. She really couldn't be any worse off. She was deluding herself if she thought things were improving, or if "professional autonomy" (which was a delusion, too) was going to be less anywhere else.

September 18

The last time Charity and Andrew went for dental check-ups, Andrew complained the entire drive. "Why do we have to do this so often? I think all this cleaning and x-raying weakens teeth, etc." Charity's dentist rarely x-rayed teeth unless there was some suspicion that he needed to. Finally Charity asked Andrew if all this complaining meant he felt guilty for not taking better care of his teeth and if he was afraid he had a cavity. "Yes," he sighed.

He didn't, but Charity, scrupulous about flossing and brushing, did.

So today, a brilliant late summer afternoon, she drove the back roads to her dentist's office. She listened to NPR, to which she was addicted. She drove slowly, the road curving through apple orchards laden with autumn fruit - a bumper crop this year, she heard on the radio. Wild asters made a riot of purple. Too gorgeous a day to be sitting in a dental chair. Charity always wondered why his office was in the middle of nowhere, or rather, in the middle of numerous apple orchards. Maybe some ancestral property called him to stay there?

Charity had a long and painful history with dentists, being prone to cavities in her younger days. She had carefully looked for and then trained her current dentist, whom she trusted implicitly. She had gone to him for nearly twenty years. "We don't use terms like pain or losing teeth," he told her early in their relationship. She had expressed a fear of dentistry in general, and needles in particular. He understood. He used nitrous oxide first, a topical anesthetic second, and, finally, the needle. If necessary, he used more Novocain. He waited for all those drugs to take effect, numbing and eliminating anxiety.

Over the years, he had had few (precious few, thank goodness!) assistants who became well-versed in the routine Charity required. Today however, there was a new assistant, who had to ask "Do you take Novocain or nitrous?" Always nitrous oxide, Charity quickly breathed. I'm afraid of needles. "Well," said Assistant soothingly, "you may not need a needle; it's only a small cavity." No Charity said, a little sharply because of her rising panic. I can't stand pain, either! Both! The dentist knows the routine!

"We'll just get you started on the nitrous, again" Assistant cooed.

When the dentist entered, smiling, (he was always smiling, Charity thought, why?) and asked how she was, she smiled back, thinking nothing personal, but I hate you. He proceeded through the routine, mentioning, "If there's any discomfort (true to his word, he never said pain) raise your finger." Charity always wanted to ask, giggling a little from the gas, which finger, doctor? When he was finished, he announced, as usual, I'm going to turn off the nitrous and you'll start feeling normal again, to which Charity invariably wanted to reply, what makes you think I ever feel normal? but she never did.

Today wasn't bad at all. She had even confirmed something she had suspected for weeks. The tooth with the cavity, in her lower molar, was connected neurologically to the above molar, which had no cavity, but was feeling twinges of pain and sensitivity. Every time he checked to see if she was numb in the affected area, she didn't feel it in that area, she felt it in the tooth above. She couldn't wait to see if getting this tooth filled alleviated the sensitivity in the one above.

After picking up her bill, she drove slowly through the countryside, numb in her lower left lip, but enjoying every minute of the beautiful ride.

September 23

Charity was learning the kids' tricks - in more ways than one. She found herself addressing her ninth graders, "Write a sentence that doesn't involve drugs or flatulence," after having too many assignments turned in involving both. They all knew what flatulence was, because Danny had asked before, "What is flatulence?" and Charity had answered, "It's passing gas." For some reason, she never thought teaching would involve such topics. Of course, that was years ago. Of course the first sentence she read in Austin's notebook for the word professional was, "Danny is a professional flatulater." She couldn't help it. She started to laugh, quietly, behind the notebook, but it increased and Jason noticed. "Hey, she's laughing over there." They all tried to guess what she found so funny, and she finally let them in on the joke. "We thought you were serious about no drugs or flatulence, so we tried to play you." I was, Charity thought, so this time the joke's on me.

Later that day, at the Motor Vehicle Bureau, she had cause to remember the kids' more trying behavior, the kind that got them labeled "emotionally disturbed," in fact, she employed it to her own ends against the bureaucracy and got the results she wanted. It seemed the petty bureaucrats who took refuge in their rules, would not allow her to register her newly purchased used car because of a discrepancy in her name. It involved an added letter on her driver's license (their mistake a year earlier) and because that didn't exactly match the name on the car registration. "Can you prove to me who you are? Do you have a birth or baptismal certificate or a marriage license with you?" the officious little clerk snipped. "I have a driver's license. It shows my name," Charity snipped right back. "But it's not the same name," chirped the clerk. "There's an extra letter in it. You have to produce identification with the same name." "It's good enough for my insurance company, my employer, and the federal social security office," said Charity, "why isn't it good enough for New York State?" "If you have a problem, you can go see someone in consultation. I can't issue a registration if your name is different on your license." "It was your office's mistake," Charity said, "I was told at the time it wouldn't be a problem. Well it is a problem but why is your mistake my problem?" "You have to discuss it with consultation. I'm not going to issue an invalid permit," the Snip said sanctimoniously, secure in her smug little cage, bound by her rules.

So Charity walked over to "Consultation." She could tell from the conversation going on with the person ahead of her that Mr. Consultation was unsympathetic, bureaucratic in the worst sense of the word, and none too intelligent. The woman turned away, after politely receiving no satisfaction. Charity stepped up, and the man's first words showed him to be a fool, and Charity did not suffer fools gladly. What he said was, "May we help you?" Since he was neither royalty, nor, she was sure, did he have a mouse in his pocket, his use of the royal "we" irritated her to the boiling point. "Yes," she said, curtly. "I am fit to be tied." She then went into a clear, chronological diatribe about the error on her license, how she had dutifully reported for a new photo, received a notice the photo machine had malfunctioned and would she come in again? She'd be given priority, they were sorry for the inconvenience, etc. They were not, she was not given priority, she had to wait in a long line and repeat the entire process and when she received her renewed license the name was recorded erroneously, and when she called they said she could come in a third time and bring proof of her actual name and they wouldn't charge her, etc, but it wouldn't be a problem for her if she left it they promised. The entire time, she was banging the documents on the desk. "So," Charity finished, "here I am, the third time I've taken off from work because of your office's incompetence, and it is a problem! As I don't intend to come back, and I do intend to register this car today, what are you going to do about it?" What he did was to immediately initial it, put her through to a clerk, and send her on her way. I didn't even curse or threaten to kill anyone, she thought, I just acted extremely edgy. She had definitely learned the uses of so-called "emotional disturbance" from the kids.

September 28

Charity was worried about Andrew. This was nothing new. She had worried about Andrew off and on, for varied and numerous reasons, since before he was born. But this time, not for the first time, Fieldlily had fed into her worries.

He cited Andrew's tendency toward dark colors and "evil" symbology in his choice of room decoration and in his own artwork. Charity had challenged Fieldlily when he brought this up. "What are you saying? Are you saying the devil has my son? Do you think he's a Satanist? Or what?" Fieldlily had looked contemptuous and said, "If that's the way you want to look at it."

Of course, Charity was concerned about Andrew's spiritual development. She was concerned about his development in all ways. She was deeply, if reticently, involved in a very mystical communication with her vision of God, and, for several visionary reasons, Mary, the Blessed Mother. So of course she wanted Andrew to develop an awareness of God and his own inner divine spark, but she had been unable to bring herself to force him into one formalized religious pattern, such as she had been brought up in.

In retrospect, she didn't think it would have been such a bad thing. It had given her a footing, a springboard, if you please, into her own deepening relationship with God.

So she worried about Andrew's soul growth. She worried about his psychological health, she worried about his physical health, drug, tobacco, alcohol use; it went on and on. Sometimes she was successful in stopping herself, reminding herself that worry was unproductive and even destructive; thinking too much about a possible negative occurrence was bound to help create an atmosphere that could make it more likely to happen. At least, that's what she believed.

So when Fieldlily, who occasionally practiced an African sort of divination, told her something had come up during a divining session, she groaned. It was inevitably serious, and usually about Andrew when he spoke like that. It was.

It seemed that Andrew was likely to be involved in a "serious," i.e. fatal, car crash unless he did one of two things: accept an initiation into Fieldlily's African-based spirituality or say a sincere prayer twice a day for guidance and protection. As he was unlikely to do either, Charity was worried, and she was worried that her worry would contribute to the danger. Of course, with him driving it was a concern, anyway. His father often expressed worry over the same thing, usually blaming Charity for allowing him to go out in cars driven by his friends. So the possibility was being heavily fed into the atmosphere.

Charity, badly wanting to dispel the notions of death and danger, urged Andrew to pray, briefly but sincerely, twice a day. He said he would. She hoped he meant it. She worried he wouldn't, as he had trouble even brushing his teeth twice a day. She explained that even if he felt it was silly, or unnecessary, or he didn't feel like it, it was a simple enough thing to do, and with a possibility of serious harm, why take a chance with your life, when the remedy was so simple? He said he would; he agreed. Charity privately thought that even if a car accident didn't happen, praying twice a day couldn't hurt, and was really encouraging what she wanted Andrew to do anyway, which was to develop a closer relationship to God.

She closed her eyes, breathed deeply, and tried to feel at peace.

September 29

The Power of the Pekingese

Fieldlily was depressed. Periodically he got depressed over his lack of income. He would mention all the things he wanted, and all the things he wanted to do, and couldn't, because of his lack of income... and he'd sink deeper into his depression. Of course, he never became sufficiently bogged down by all of this to actually go out and get a job. That would be taking it into realms that were definitely beyond Fieldlily's capacity.

When Charity got home from the Academy and when she had finished with the hour-plus massage therapy appointment she did regularly every Monday, Fieldlily began his litany:

He was depressed.

He hated the area.

He couldn't find a guru here.

There were no jobs for him available.

He needed to study more and he couldn't find teachers he was willing to learn from.

Etc etc.

Charity usually tuned him out, but today he seemed so down that she decided to employ "the Power of the Pekingese."

Maggie, or Magdalena B. Lee, was a purebred Pekingese puppy that Charity had been given by her friend Ruby, who raised them. On the day Charity brought Maggie home, she had dropped off the puppy and headed to work at the hotel. Fieldlily protested.

"I didn't think you were really going to get another pet. I'm not sure I want it keeping me up at night. I..."

Charity left, and when she returned, hours later, Fieldlily met her at the door with an enraptured expression.

"I've been with the puppy all day!" He grinned foolishly, totally besotted.

Maggie had completely charmed him. And when she was quickly housebroken and did not, in fact, whine or bark at night, or any other time for that matter, Fieldlily was won over entirely.

"It's my baby-dog!" He would coo at her. "Come here, little bumblebee-head."

So when he was stressed or upset or down, Charity would place Maggie on his lap and, wonder of wonders, where he used to become irritated at her mere mention of the pets when he was in emotional crisis, he would now melt, pull out of his despondency and begin to croon and play with the puppy. Charity had never seen him like this.

The Power of the Pekingese was a very strong power, indeed.

October 9

Charity often felt like she wanted to escape to another country. The crime, waste, pollution and spiritual bankruptcy of America seemed overwhelming, and from what she had heard and read about say, Europe, it seemed much less problematic. Of course, she had never even visited Europe, so she didn't really know, but Americans had a history of being expatriates, and the concept romantically appealed to Charity, especially when she felt overwhelmed. Realistically, however, she realized that the world's problems were global and merely moving to another country wouldn't change anything. Still the thoughts persisted. Were murders less frequent in Britain? Was France less polluted, did Spain have better weather, could she really learn a language fluently by living in the country where it was spoken?

October 12

As Charity wrote the date in her journal, she reflected what it meant to her. She knew it was the date that marked Columbus' arrival in the New World... Arrival after deceiving his crew, after enduring hardships caused by the extended weeks, he having, of course, miscalculated the distance; arrival just as the crew was just about to mutiny. Having grown up in Columbus, Ohio, Charity was well steeped in the Columbus legend.

But... having Cherokee ancestry, from her mother, who grew up in Tennessee, in the Smokey Mountains, sacred to the Cherokee, Charity was also aware of what today meant to her pre-Columbian ancestors, and what it meant to the indigenous peoples in "the New World," and that was the beginning of the end: decimation of entire peoples, death, disease, destruction of their way of life. Charity had once attended a workshop lead by a Lakota Nation elder (an education workshop, which the Academy encouraged its teachers to attend!) and he had mentioned in his key note address, how all the negatives in the English language seem to begin with the letter d. Looking at her list of what Columbus' arrival portended, she decided that today, celebrated as "Columbus Day," was the real D-day.

October 13

Charity's dreams, when asleep, were taking a bizarre bent toward the mundane, and they all involved the staff and/or kids at the Academy. The night before last, she dreamed that the former teacher in the self-contained class, of all people, was in Charity's basement doing, of all things, her laundry! Last night she dreamed that the music therapist/teacher, and a young assistant, had moved into an apartment together for financial reasons, and when Charity asked how they were getting along, the musician said, "Ok, but one of his legs is shorter than the other, and he doesn't brush his teeth." What was she to make of these dreams, which only indirectly involved her?

October 14

Charity decided, after being a passenger in a car driven by Andrew, that her idea of Hell was being a passenger in a car, driven too fast for her comfort, and with loud, unsettling, demonic-sounding music blaring accompaniment. The realization made her giggle, nervously, and she said as much to Andrew.

October 15

Fourth period English class, which was inhabited by the second group of eighth graders, but who were all older than regular eighth graders, was a trial for Charity, especially coming as it did right before lunch. For instance, today they were looking up vocabulary words that should have been completed yesterday, and it was looking every bit like they would not even complete it today, since the period was already half over, and they were generally daydreaming, talking about completely unrelated topics, and doing everything but writing down definitions. Sam, who wore glasses which at least made him appear scholarly, was leafing through the dictionary and stopping wherever he found a picture of an animal, then making a comment about it. When he came on a buffalo, he asked, "Will a buffalo come after you and attack you?" (So much violence in these boys' conversation, in their lives, Charity thought.)

As she was reflecting, Ryan answered for her, "Yes, they will, if you go up to them and say your mother!"

"They do?" Sam asked, wide-eyed and gullible, "they understand you?"

"Yes," said Ryan, simply, chortling to himself at his cleverness.

"Really?" Sam asked Charity, "They really will?"

"Well, only if you shout it at them," Charity said, going along with the joke to Ryan's amazement.

She reflected again at how the words were such potent instigators to all the boys at the Academy. They were just words, until one boy shouted them at another and then they were a call to arms.

Charity recalled the insults being leveled at one another in her junior high school days, but it was more of a joke in her peer group. "Yo mamma!" They'd say to each other, or "Your mother wears combat boots!" and laugh hysterically.

Not these kids. They wanted to fight - it was an insult, a challenge. The notion of one kid catching on to the absurdity of it enough to imagine it setting off a buffalo was truly funny and witty.

"They look so friendly in the picture," Sam said.

October 18

It was Saturday...

Andrew's car, the second car, the one Charity had bought with money she really didn't have but scraped together anyway, the one Andrew drove more than anyone, wouldn't start. It had already cost almost half of its purchase price to get on the road, and now it wouldn't start. The car Charity had taken of the road in order to transfer the plates and registration and be able to afford the insurance, the one Andrew refused to learn to drive, because it was a standard shift, still started perfectly. The (very expensive) local mechanic said it was no problem; he'd come over late morning and as he put it address the problem. "No reason not to do it today," he said. No reason at all, thought Charity, for you. It's only money I don't have. "What are your labor rates these days?" She ventured. "About $50," he said cheerfully. About? Charity was thinking, "Really $49" he finished. Great, a bargain. Not even $50 an hour.

Charity reflected on what she earned an hour:

When she did private massage clients at home, it was $35 to $50 an hour. There were very few of these lately, for many reasons, not the least of which was what her therapist termed a "force field" around the house created by Fieldlily.

When she worked at the hotel, which she would probably do today, what with the car needing attention and money for the attention, and since Sophia the receptionist had already called her to see if she was available, she got $37.50 an hour, $35 after taxes. Sometimes the guests there gave her tips, more often lately they did not. The hotel had recently been sold and there was talk of a raise $5 per appointment, but so far that wasn't the case.

The Academy, which talked about yearly salaries, in actuality behaved and functioned like it was an hourly wage. Based on yearly hours worked, and what their rate was for after school tutoring, Charity figured her hourly rate there was about $16 before taxes.

A dozen years ago, when she was doing several things to earn money and stay home, her hourly massage rate was $25, she got paid $15 an hour to teach children's dance classes, and $20 an hour to do home tutoring for the local public school.

When she was a teenager, she made $15 an hour modeling for local stores and ads in her hometown. This was thirty years ago, give or take a year or two.

This slow financial degradation just didn't make sense. A recent slang expression was "go figure." That's just what Charity was trying to do. The figures just weren't working out, and it was depressing.

October 21

Charity was thinking a lot lately about the passage of time. She supposed this was because, at 46, she was actually middle-aged, although she felt exactly like she did in graduate school or just after. Fifteen years ago, at 30, she felt the same way.

Some of this line of thought was aided by receiving a statement of her pension plan at an Academy staff meeting. It projected her net worth at a retirement age of 65. Charity realized with a start that 65 was only nineteen years away, and that in nineteen years she would be old, not middle-aged. This caused her to think back nineteen years, when she was 25, which actually was a young adult. She remembered anxiously looking for the first signs of wrinkles. There weren't any, but she imagined there were. She had no children then, but she was teaching at the Academy which was just the plain Boys Home then. She had left, vowing not to return, but she obviously had.

She had no new car then, and no debt, either. She was married to Andrew's father, and had high hopes of having a medium-sized family and owning a big, old house. She loved living in an area rich in history, and being close to Andrew's father's family, who lived an hour and a half away, and vacationed and then retired on Cape Cod. Now, as many years forward as that time was past, she was peeking into her own possible retirement, and all that had changed irrevocably.

October 22

"If you give to charity, give with all your heart." New English Bible, Romans chapter 12, verse 8.

Charity awoke sick, something that rarely happened to her. It had been coming on for a few days, but this morning it was full blown. Her head ached, her throat was scratchy, she had a post-nasal drip and a fever. She wanted to go back to bed, especially when she realized she had to arrange a ride because Fieldlily needed the car and the other car would not start.

When she arrived at the Academy, after getting a ride with her friend Hope, she really wished she had stayed at home, because her assistant was out, the kids were rowdy, she felt ill, and, in their mailboxes, the Academy staff received additions to their staff handbooks. The handbooks, called such because the office carp, who was a high school dropout, couldn't manage a word like manual, were supposed to detail policies and procedures. Actually, it only outlined these things, because they were written by the office carp, see above, and the additions were used by said office carp to vent her spleen about personal grievances directed at the staff in general and general resentments pointed at specific people for whom she bore a misplaced grudge.

October 25

Charity was helping Grace pack to move to North Carolina. She couldn't believe it. Grace was leaving the Academy. Not that Charity blamed her. Charity was glad for her and admired her courage. Grace had been "reprimanded" and suspended for two days without pay, without warning, unfairly, for a theft by a student (the radio stolen had been returned.) No student would own up to it, so Grace, who had done the exact thing she was supposed to do in such circumstances, had been suspended. Charity suspected the office carp had goaded the school directors into this - it had her signature all over it; spiteful, the sneaky surprise attack that hit where it most hurt, with the low salaries at the Academy. How petty! How mean! Charity seethed. But Grace rose above it, went to North Carolina where she had friends and where her son had spent the summer, and then and there planned a move, within a month.

October 28

Charity had felt on the verge of crying for days. But the tears wouldn't come, just hovered below the surface. She still felt ill, and overwhelmed. Andrew's car broke down again. Fieldlily insisted an acquaintance and former client of his could fix it, but then wouldn't call him for one reason or another.

Andrew needed to take his driving test, there was no car for him, and when Charity tried to contact a mechanic, whose fee was something like fifty dollars an hour, both Fieldlily and Andrew said they knew someone who could fix it, don't spend that kind of money. Meanwhile, Fieldlily said, pulling a long face, his car needed fixing. Actually, it was Charity's car, but she rarely drove it. Fieldlily needed to get out and do his (mostly pointless) errands, see his therapist, attend whatever meditation or spiritual study group had his attention for the moment. Charity often thought to herself that he subscribed to the "Religion of the Month" club. So she rode with a colleague who had once asked "is Felipe a Buddhist?" And Charity had slipped and said her quip about the Religion of the Month club. Charity would insist that Fieldlily do errands, or take Andrew to school. It was her car, after all, and she paid all the bills on it. Transporting her son was the least Fieldlily could do, she felt.

Now that Andrew's car was out of commission, and he had a road test scheduled, Charity tried to rent a car from "Cheap Heap," but they had none available. They suggested she call a rental company not far away, but when she did, their terms were either a major credit card or a seven hundred dollar cash deposit. Charity, always on the edge financially, had recently joined Debtors Anonymous and cut up all her credit cards, so this was not a viable option. She called a final budget rental company whom she had rented a car from nine years before, and they said major credit cards were the way they usually operated, but they did have a cash procedure, it just took longer and they ran a credit check. She hung up the phone, and Fieldlily said, "Instead of renting a car, why not take the forty dollars and use it toward fixing Andrew's car? He can postpone the driving test." Charity felt like he was continually throwing obstacles in her path when she tried to take action. She felt like crying. A credit check! Fix the old car! Who? When? Postpone, put off, make do. Overwhelming. Like the piles of laundry, mail, and recycling. Every time she had a free day from the Academy or hotel work, she wanted to use the time to tackle the clutter in the bedroom, but Fieldlily would insist on going somewhere and she would be prevented. Last Sunday, when Fieldlily went to see his latest guru-lama or somebody in the small-town Arts community near them that Fieldlily frequented far too much for someone who said he loathed the place, she had attacked her closet and some of the bedroom clutter. She was overwhelmed half way through the day, and felt like crying, but didn't. When Fieldlily got home, he even joined her and put away some of his clutter.

Charity Begins at Home

Later that week, the same day she had attempted a car rental, in fact, Charity had taken a group of students to what she hoped was the last visit to the Farm that season. It was cold, as it had been last week, and she felt ill. Her eyes burned and she could barely breathe. Driving the van back to the Academy, she told the kids to put on their seatbelts. Most of them did, but Jason, who just had to be oppositional, it was part of his spiritual discipline, Charity felt sure, did not, refused, in fact, and when a truck with a faulty brake light suddenly stopped in front of them, Charity slammed on the brakes, and Jason went flying. "I hit my head! You're trying to kill us!" He screamed, "My back hurts! I wasn't sitting up." Charity felt like saying, "I told you so," and also like crying, in equal proportions. This Farm trip was never fun for her, and it was such a foolish idea on the Academy's part and so poorly thought out!

October 31

"I'm a shadow of my former self," Charity said to the mirror. I feel so old, so heavy - I've gained weight - so ungraceful. I feel so unattractive. At even 42 or 43, she had still felt young, lively, pretty. Now she felt aged, tired, faded, sexless. Well, she was sexless, Fieldlily having decided he was too sensitive for physical intimacy.

The young women she worked with at the Academy certainly didn't help. Clothes, make-up, all things superficial were what obsessed them, and the education of anyone - themselves or the Academy kids - was the last thing on their shallow minds.

She hadn't felt well for over a week, she was on her period, and she supposed this affected her mood and her self-esteem, but still, when she was like this, she wondered if she would ever feel energetic, or happy, or nice-looking, or just plain good again.

November 9

Charity made a list of things she detested:

She detested herbal tea in the morning, especially if she hadn't yet had any caffeine.

She detested - to the point that it made her angry to smell it - Champa incense.

She detested people who were trying to be politically correct, and who had no Indian ancestry, going out of their way to say Native American. For that matter, she detested people going out of their way to say African American when she could tell they were agonizing over the words, in painfully correct use. Once, when she was thinking about her own ancestors, a voice had come into her head with the clear statement, "We'd prefer, if you have to call us anything, to be called pre-Americans."

She detested anyone calling her home for business, political, or telemarketing purposes, asking for her by her first name, as if they were old acquaintances and they weren't calling for money or a vote.

"Charity?" They would ask, and she would say, "who?" And they would say, "Charity," and she would ask who was calling, and why, and they would be forced to say it, and she would say, "I don't know you, do I?" And they would be thrown off their prepared speech, and she'd say, "If this isn't a personal call, you really need to use my surname," knowing most of the little chirps hired for phoning probably didn't know what a surname was, and by then they would be completely thrown off course and Charity, having made her point, would say goodbye sweetly and hang up.

Charity detested being called "Chare," in particular and nicknames in general.

She detested hearing people chew or swallow near her.

She detested people whistling or clapping too loudly near her ears.

November 10

Every year around Veteran's Day, Charity had the tenth graders read a short story by Tim O'Brien about the Viet Nam War, "The Things They Carried," and then showed a documentary about that war, called "Dear American."

She had lived through the war, through most of Junior High, all of High School and college, and most of graduate school. She had watched the daily casualties on the evening news, heard reports of former high school friends sent over. During her freshman year of college, the government eliminated student deferments and instituted the lottery, whereby her male classmates could be drafted immediately if they pulled the wrong number based on their birthdays. When the war escalated, students and professors began to protest, joining the Quakers, conscientious objectors and others who objected to war in general. In the spring of her freshman year, Charity joined the protest in the streets of her college town, and when the National Guard was called in, she watched in horror as her fellow students were shot on the campus, and all the schools in the state were shut down for summer break early.

So she had deep, emotional involvement in the Viet Nam War, and she was always a little hesitant to teach about it for fear the students would react the way they usually did: disinterested, disrespectfully commenting on whatever reading material she chose, or completely refusing to do anything at all. Especially the tenth grade group this year. All they seemed to care about was procuring illegal drugs and arguing with each other.

So it was with hesitation that she introduced the story that week before Veteran's Day.

To her grateful astonishment, nobody said what are we reading this for or this is whacked, this is boring, they read it avidly, asking all kinds of questions, asking could they read more, find out more? Charity hadn't even had to preface it with this war was my generation's war, it means a lot to me, I lost friends to this war. She hadn't had to say any of it. They were caught; they were interested. No one even interrupted to ask to get a drink or a restroom pass, a sure sign that they were getting bored. They read it through to the end, which took two days, without any disruptions or unrelated comments, a major feat for this class of reluctant readers.

So Charity had rented the Dear America video and shown it. Even though she had previewed it at home, she was worried she might tear up. Viet Nam stories did that to her. The whole era had shaped her so much emotionally and politically. Worse, she was afraid they'd make joking comments and she'd lose her temper.

But when she put the video on, and the introduction explained this was actual footage from the war not a re-enactment, and she had explained this was the first war where news people had actually gone into battle zones to be killed alongside soldiers, they were silent. They only asked serious, genuine questions. When it was over, there was an eerie silence in the room. In a hush, they filed out, collecting their papers.

"I'm sorry," Rick whispered to her. "Sorry you had to go through that."

November 20

Trouble in Paradise

It had been a long day. Charity had arrived late to find her assistant was also late, which meant the assistant principal, Ms. Chambers, was sitting behind the desk, minding the homeroom. It looked bad, and it was the second time she had been late that week, so it looked really bad. "Well, you were only seven or eight minutes late," Sam had commented. "That's not so bad." Charity realized the main draw to working at the Academy was the kids. Never mind that later that morning, just before lunch, low blood sugar must play a part in this, Charity guessed, Sam, for no known reason, suddenly began slamming Jason's head into the chalkboard, over and over. Charity felt unnerved. It had apparently been a bad morning for her entire homeroom, and nine voices had been clamoring for her undivided attention. Not to mention a colleague who poked her head in the door to inquire, not what all the fuss was, but "Why is that child sitting at a teacher's desk?" The "child" in question was seventeen years old and six feet two inches, had asked for permission, and was quietly doing vocabulary work.

To be policed by colleagues addressing irrelevant minutiae while kids were being hurt - really! Charity fumed inwardly. It was too much!

Plus, she had lunch duty. And overdue paperwork to do during her "prep" period.

After lunch, one student touched her hand when she was handing out pencils and asked, "Why is your hand so warm?"

I must have a fever, she thought. I'll have to take it when I get home. But before she could go home, she had to finish her paperwork, deposit her paycheck in the bank, put gas in the car, and get to the post office before it closed to mail the overdue rent, phone, and electric payments, which meant she was then out of money, so she couldn't buy heating oil for another two weeks, if then.

By the time she got home, Fieldlily was in a state. "5:00! Where have you been? Why didn't you call? I've been stuck here all day and Andrew couldn't let me use his car because he had to go somewhere after school. What's with that anyway? I hate this lack of clarity! Is it only his car? Isn't he supposed to use it only to go to and from school? You have to put your foot down!" (This was coincidentally what her mother had told Charity last Sunday on the phone when Charity had said Fieldlily had no job yet.) "I was stuck inside all day! I hate it here!" He went on this way for sometime before Charity could interject a word, asking him if he'd like to come with her now to return some library books and look for some others. He went, but fumed at her the whole way. "I don't want to stay too long! I need air! I want exercise! I couldn't go anywhere today, because I didn't have the car!" He had had the car for the previous two days.

He also absolutely refused to walk down the road in their rural neighborhood.

Charity looked for books on Viet Nam and the Kent State shootings that she had promised to her students. Fieldlily read the newspaper. When Charity couldn't find the books she needed right away and went to consult the card catalog, she noticed him looking for books in the stacks. Good, I have some more time, she thought. He came up to her and showed her two books he was taking out. She smiled and went to get the books she wanted. When she fumbled with one, trying to find the information in its index unsuccessfully, Fieldlily tossed his books impatiently and went to reshelve them. "Wait! I'm done now." She said, "Don't you want them?" "I'm not really interested in them!" He hissed.

The whole evening he had behaved like a petulant child, taking out his boredom on her, being short-tempered, never once asking her how her day had gone.

When they finally got home, Charity offered to make something to eat. "No! I'm not hungry!" he snapped. What about the flan she had made last night? "It's from a package! My mother would say (something in Spanish for junk) and never even buy it at the store!"

Charity snapped. It was way too much. "You! I made it for you, I tried, I told you I knew it wasn't authentic from scratch, I know it's not what your mother would make! I never pretended it was! I'm exhausted when I get home and I take short cuts cooking. So don't have any! Just stop complaining! You never once asked me how my day was. Well, it was pretty terribly lousy! Now, take the car and go somewhere and stop criticizing me! I've had enough of that, and being yelled at, from students and colleagues today!"

Fieldlily backed down. She had beaten him at his game. It was the second time that day that she had stepped out of her calm demeanor to shout down a hyperactive Hispanic. The first was one of her homeroom students who would habitually misbehave and then go AWOL from the room and go sulk somewhere to avoid facing the music. Today she hadn't let that happen. She had followed him, chased him down, haranguing him the whole way. He finally gave up and came back and behaved reasonably well the rest of the day.

"Well, I wasn't yelling at you," Fieldlily said.

"I didn't say you were," Charity said, "I'm just tired of your complaints." Fieldlily was quiet for a while. Before he left, he said, "Thanks for hearing all my complaints."

He left. It was 8:15 p.m... Charity, still feeling ill, took her temperature. She had a fever.

She felt like crying, she felt like crying, she felt like crying.

November 22

Charity felt disappointed. It was the Saturday before Thanksgiving and she had been hoping from the day off from the hotel health club, since most likely people would be going to the hotel the following weekend for the long holiday. Plus, as the third person on call, it was really unlikely she would work. So she planned to shop and gather a bag of groceries for the local food pantry. She felt drawn to do this every year, and she missed the Boy Scout food drive again! She planned to drop the groceries off along with some used but good clothing. Then, in the afternoon, she planned to go to a Gallery opening to see two of her women friends' artwork.

All that changed, as she deep down knew it inevitably would. Marney called. Her father, who was 85, was in the hospital again, and she felt she needed to be near the phone that day. Would Charity cover for her at the hotel? Appealed to this way, of course she would. It could be her early holiday sacrifice she thought. Marney then told her that since the hotel had changed hands, they were starting to implement some changes, one being that Sophia had been moved to another position and there was a new, young, very inexperienced woman there now. This was somewhat disturbing news, as in the past new receptionists had botched bookings, and vouchers, and they had lost pay and clients as a result.

When the new person then called Charity to confirm she was covering for Marney, Charity was convinced that this was a potential disaster in the making. She had booked her for one half hour in the middle of the day, making it impossible to do anything before or after. Nothing more was available "as of now." Charity tried to explain that she needed more than a half hour, that it took her an hour to get there, and she also needed to be called an hour ahead to have time to make it. The girl was distracted (Charity remembered she had additional duties that Sophia had not had) and barely listened. "Karen booked the half hour," was all she said, and hung up. Karen was the head masseuse, and Charity knew it was a lie. Damn!

It was still too early to take a shower. Fieldlily had not slept well and she didn't want the noise to wake him. He had been awakened in the middle of the night by the pets and had awakened Charity with his complaints, said in a very hateful way and directed at her: his need for sleep, his ongoing illnesses, her fault for bringing new pets into the environment when he said he didn't want them, how this was a nightly occurrence, etc, etc. Charity commented that he was being hateful to her and that he had always had sleeping problems even before the new pets, or even before knowing her, that he was a miserable person and that it had nothing to do with the pets.

Fieldlily seemed pleased to be described as hateful and miserable and commented back to her, with renewed enthusiasm, that what his complaint was tonight was the new pets waking him up at night, and Charity was always changing the subject, even though she knew it aggravated him, etc.

Charity responded by saying she was sorry her extraneous desire for pets had interfered with his legitimate health concern of not getting enough sleep. She wasn't being sarcastic. She could see that one was a necessity and one was a desire.

Mollified, Fieldlily promptly went back to sleep, but Charity heard the pets start playing noisily again, and she got up to distract and quiet them. It was now early morning, so she stayed up and sat in the kitchen, writing in her journal. She wrote about the latest skirmish with Fieldlily. Then she realized and wrote down how miserable she was. She worked sometimes seven days a week. She still couldn't make ends meet. Her only pair of shoes had a big hole in them. She was still running a fever. She couldn't afford a haircut and her hair looked awful, especially after she had caught one side on fire, singeing and thinning it. She was lucky she wasn't bald or burned, she knew. But it contributed to her sense of sadness. She put down the pen, put her head down on the table, and started to cry.

She became aware of something warm and soft by her foot, looked down and saw Maggie through her tears. She picked her up, and the little Pekingese started to lick the tears as they fell on her cheeks. This made Charity cry even more, for a different reason. Another power of the Pekingese was the power to intuit when comfort was needed. Oh, Maggie!

November 26

As the day before Thanksgiving approached, Charity woke at dawn with a cramp in her gut and a pain in her back and she realized she had started her period. She remembered that her first period had started on Thanksgiving Day when she was 12. 30 plus years of periods! One a month, very regularly except when she had been pregnant. All this for one child!

As her cramps worsened - it was one of those months – she recalled conversations over the years with other women about periods in general, and cramps specifically. There seemed to be two camps, with variations. The "I hate my period, period" group, and the "I never get cramps," or a worse variation on that, "I love it! I am participation in Mother Earth's mysteries!" The latter group gloried in their "monthly power time" or their "moons." (Charity wondered just how many of them had pre-American heritage, that they could blithely borrow the terminology.) Another variant in this group was those insensitive souls who would ask Charity how she could complain about cramps when she had a baby? Apparently, childbirth had cured *them*, so it was universal. She hated comments like that, and also any suggestion that she was creating her own cramps because she was not in tune with her own womanhood. Charity had very little use for such judgmental personalities. She much preferred her friend Ruby, who had four children and who still regularly got cramps. She recommended lying down with a heating pad, taking ginger tea or aspirin, or both. She never mouthed such sentiments as one should never suffer cramps again after the glories of childbirth or the recognition of one's earthy nature as a bleeding goddess.

It was not that Charity did not acknowledge that it was a natural, healthy part of womanhood. She just didn't like pain, and she meant pain. Her friend Alexandra had once mentioned how she dealt with "the discomfort" by making her own moon ritual, and she suggested Charity do the same for "the discomfort." "Alexandra, I'm talking about pain," Charity sighed, realizing that Alexandra was in the Earth Mysteries camp and could never understand.

November 30

Advent Conversation

It was the first Sunday in Advent, according to the Christian Church Calendar, the start of the Christmas season, the fifth season of the year, that time between autumn and winter that was its own special time.

As Charity reviewed the wants of the season (gifts, a tree, cards, baking) along with the necessities (fuel oil for heating, and now, it seemed, lp gas for cooking, as it was running out, ahead of schedule, car insurance - on both cars - past due electric bills and, of course, rent, phone, and regular expenses) it became painfully evident that, once again, the wants would come up lacking. She made her secret wish list anyway. You never know. Charity believed in Christmas miracles. She believed that if she gave what she could to those in greater need, even if it meant a sacrifice in one way or another, that she would receive what she truly needed and desired, in some mysterious, miraculous, alchemically metaphysical way.

Meanwhile, it just felt like an uphill battle, and not miraculous at all. She was forever trying to bring the spiritual aspect of the season into focus and to counteract the obscene commercial overtaking of it, not only for herself, but for Andrew. She felt like she was losing the battle. Not that Andrew was especially material, he wasn't, but he wasn't especially spiritual, either, at least not that Charity could see. Since she had been told by a psychic, who was a devout Christian as well, that Andrew was "a very spiritual child," she could only hope that adolescence was obscuring it for the time being.

So, it was Christmas season, officially and Charity swung into gear: she began by praying and trying to feel grateful on Thanksgiving. She had worked two days at the hotel over Thanksgiving weekend, usually a mixed blessing, as it meant long days but lucrative ones. This year it was not so lucrative, that had been the trend for a while, but Charity realized something, a realization that overtook her before she was aware of it, it was so subtle about slowly creeping into her being.

She felt better.

She didn't feel tired, or achy, or depressed. She felt - hopeful. And not worried anymore, not upset with Fieldlily, not even disturbed by her mother's latest phone call.

That call had come earlier in the day, and her mother had begun as usual by asking Charity how she was and then without waiting for her answer going on to tell Charity how she was, and the various states of health, usually poor, of their various former neighbors with whom her mother kept in touch religiously. She then went on to ask about Charity's finances, was she set with heat for the winter? How was her old car holding up? Since she wasn't offering any monetary assistance, Charity was usually irritated and somewhat hurt by this stage in their habitual conversation.

Charity Begins at Home

When her mother asked about finances, she was really asking if Fieldlily had a job yet. She hadn't caught on yet, that Fieldlily wasn't going to get a job, not ever.

But since Charity was feeling better, she just calmly answered that, no, she didn't have heat yet, it was a good thing the temperature had been mild, and the old car was doing as well as could be expected. Then her mother indirectly commented about Fieldlily, admonishing Charity, once again, to "Put her foot down." She went on to say, "Well, there are alternatives, but I don't suppose you want to do that." Charity felt so much better, she felt mischievous.

"Why, Mother, are you suggesting murder?" She asked.

Charity's mother said goodbye rather quickly.

Charity smiled.

December 3

Everything was getting on her nerves:

The kids fooling around, and then becoming defiant and hostile when Charity reprimanded them.

Fellow teachers being more concerned with Charity's enforcement of irrelevant rules, (there were irrelevant rules and important rules, like writing passes to the water fountain - irrelevant - not like no punching each other - important) rather than if there was any learning going on.

Office and assistant staff - what the school psychologist called "the little girls" - being terribly concerned about the apparel of the entire staff, their make-up and hair styles, or, horrors! The lack thereof!

Women her age, at the hotel, at dance class, talking incessantly about menopause symptoms and "the aging process." Aging! (Her mother at 79 didn't talk about "the aging process" and probably didn't at Charity's age, either.)

Fieldlily's list of complaints, which increased like the loaves and fishes, at a ratio of about 2:1; every time she addressed one complaint, he had two more to take its place.

December 6

Sometimes, Charity felt like she was trying desperately to hold on, to hold everything together, to hold on to things.

She held on to Andrew, trying desperately to keep him safe, to help with his future direction.

She tried to hold it together at the Academy, trying to keep the kids working on their education and their behavior, and trying, always, to satisfy the ever-increasing rules, which were established because the administration too felt out of control.

She tried to hold the line financially, trying to pay bills, trying to stay on top of things, trying not to spend, trying to economize.

She tried to hold on to her health and fitness by dancing, taking supplements and eating right.

She sometimes wondered how she could hold a single thing more, without dropping them all, like when she went shopping for just a few groceries, so she wouldn't use a cart, and then she'd reach for one more thing, and drop the whole armful.

She wondered why she kept trying to hold on at all – why didn't she just drop the whole load? And not take on, or try to hold onto, anything more?

December 11

'Tis the Season...

It was the season, and Charity wondered how she could manage to pay all her bills on time (and she was already late with the rent... again!) and still have anything left for Christmas, now just two weeks away. She would have to be very, very creative, or very, very miserly, Scrooge-like, even, to manage at all.

Meanwhile, the heating oil and cooking gas had run out simultaneously, car insurance was due, and the Pekingese went into early heat. She kept attacking the big Chow, Malcolm, (who had never been fixed, for reasons Charity had trouble reconciling), as if to say, "I'm in heat, and what are you going to *do* about it, big boy?" hanging from his ruff and growling. Malcolm, who weighed 90 pounds, would sit up, shaking her off his neck, looking completely confused. Maggie took to stalking Cherokee, the new male kitten, who was just as confused as Malcolm at being on the receiving end of all this female aggression, and from a foreign species, no less!

Charity didn't even feel like decorating the house this year, one of her antidotes to seasonal depression and destitution, in part because she knew the two new kittens, who weren't even three months old, would trash the ornaments even as Charity put them up. Selene, the female, was particularly vicious. She, too, would ambush Malcolm, all 12 ounces of her. Charity shuttered to think what she could do to a fully laden Christmas tree.

It didn't matter - she hadn't had a traditional tree for four years, since her sister had invaded her home with her family and her fundamentalist Christian ideals and, shocked at Fieldlily's various religious shrines, and denying Charity's very real complaints about their mutual family of origin, had picked a nasty fight with Charity and Fieldlily and had left at 12:30 am Christmas morning. She insisted on trying to run Charity's household the way she, Chloe, had thought it should be, and refused to hear any and all discussion or reason as to why she was being impossible.

Since that time, Charity could barely stand to talk to her, although she did, occasionally, after Chloe had apologized (hollowly, Charity felt, since she thought Chloe felt she had God on only her, Chloe's, side) and Charity still could not bring herself to have a Christmas tree and could only just manage to celebrate Christmas in her own way. She had always felt despondent at this time of year, but she tried to fight it with seasonal lights and faith in miracles. This year, she just didn't feel up to the battle and she couldn't really hold Fieldlily, the original Grinch and/or seasonal depressive, or her sister responsible.

Still, she couldn't help indulging in a bit of the "if only's"

If only the Academy suddenly, miraculously, for the first time, handed out a Christmas bonus!

If only her mother would send her a Christmas check, early, so Charity could buy gifts for others with it.

If only her bills could be less, Fieldlily had some income, she didn't choose to participate at all in any holiday activities!

If only!

December 13

Oh, No...

It was 6:00 am and Maggie had eeped - once - but it was enough to awaken Fieldlily, who had a field day with Charity over it.

"I have a sore throat. I need my sleep. I got to bed late. You know I'm a light sleeper. You don't understand. Now I have to go back to sleep until 12:00 or 1:00 and I wanted to do things tomorrow..."

Charity ignored him. Any suggestions she might make now would bring on a tirade. It was her fault. It was always her fault. Her fault he was sick. Her fault he was a light sleeper. Her fault for bringing in the pets.

Her fault, she reflected, for marrying him. That was a fact. That was the central issue. Why did she continue to put up with it? What was it costing her, not just in terms of what damages he had done to the house and its contents, not just in terms of her being the sole breadwinner, and paying for his therapy, herbal medications, and initiations, not just in those terms; what about her own health and well being?

Charity Begins at Home

As Andrew would say, "think about it, Mom... He doesn't work. He can sleep all day if he wants to. The least he can do is the dishes once in a while. Or, if he can't handle that, he can at least give you respect for supporting him."

Out of the mouths of (almost) babes! "Think about it, Mom..." Charity muttered to herself.

December 15

No season made Charity feel lonelier, sadder, or more ragged than Christmas. This year seemed to be worse than most. Fieldlily staged daily tirades about his ill-health and Charity's contributions to it, especially her "selfish" insistence on keeping pets. "Too many pets!" He would declare and stomp off. "And the heat in this house! It's the worst - all that dust irritates my allergies!" He hadn't worked in nearly three years, except very sporadically and any money he got he immediately spent on himself in an effort to help alleviate his pain, discomfort and despondency.

So Charity had worked two jobs, one full time at the Academy, one part time at the hotel, and struggled to make ends meet. This year ends were meeting even less than usual. The gap between what was owed and what she earned was wider than it had ever been.

She had tried to economize. She tried to be creative. She tried to keep her spirits up. She failed.

She, who received so many positive comments about how good she made people feel after one of her massage sessions, had not had any massage work in four years.

She hadn't had a hair cut, a new pair of shoes, or any new clothes, especially winter wear, for two or more years. Her only pair of gloves had been stolen by a student at the Academy. Her last pair of shoes had a hole in them. Her boots sprung a leak, and had been patched, but were still pretty shabby.

So she felt ragged, and poor, and she didn't know how she was going to afford any Christmas presents this year.

Fieldlily said he didn't need any. He had bought himself a $40 book with money a friend had repaid him for collect phone calls. The trouble was, it was on her phone bill, that she had paid. Why couldn't Fieldlily ever consider that she might want a small gift once in a while?

She had to get something for Andrew - he couldn't be ignored at Christmas - and shouldn't be. She could send cards to her family. God knows, they usually ignored her.

She wanted to give to community, church, or human services groups like she did every year, and she didn't know how she could. All these charities advertised for donations especially this time of year, and Charity wanted to help. But Charity was never eligible for any charity herself.

December 16

The week before Christmas, Charity announced to her classes that they would be reading the play version of "A Christmas Carol." The students, she was gratified to note, were enthusiastic: I wanna be Bob Marley! I wanna be the Christmas presents! Scrooge! I wanna be Scrooge!

Charity assigned parts and they began reading. "That's not a booming voice!" Danny yelled, when one student read his part in a monotone. A few students read in Cockney accents. They were very convincing, Charity thought, but some of the kids didn't. "That's wacked! You're crazy!" They said. Kevin read the part of Tiny Tim. He was small, hyperactive, impulsive, so of course he kept screaming, "God bless us, everyone!" at regular, unscripted intervals. Marvin read the part of the Ghost of Christmas Future, who had no lines but only pointed. Every time the narrator read about the phantom pointing, Marvin raised his hand, only, and barely indicated an area to his right, no matter what the stage directions said. He did it exactly the same way each time, and each time it seemed funnier.

Charity could hardly contain her laughter. They were certainly dramatic. It was type casting.

December 27

Charity sat in her favorite chair in her favorite room, the dining room. It was two days after Christmas, and she was still processing this grim occasion. It helped to reread "Were the Ornaments Lovely?" in one of her favorite books <u>Do the Windows Open?</u> by Julie Hecht. The author seemed to have a cheerfully resigned attitude toward the holidays, expecting them to be rather awful, and not at all like "normal American holidays." Charity felt this was much more realistic. She shared a conviction with the author that normal American family life was a mystery to be pondered, pursued like a koan. What is normal American family life, especially during holidays?

It certainly wasn't what went on in her home. This year she didn't even decorate, did not even put a few miniature ornaments on her Norfolk Island pine tree. It was looking too unhealthy. Charity suspected the kittens had used it as a second litter pan. Andrew said he didn't care if they had a tree or not. His father was pressing him to go there for Christmas Eve and Christmas Day. Andrew agreed grudgingly, but Charity could tell he didn't really want to. "I hate family dinners," he said.

Charity hadn't even shopped or planned for a Christmas meal, and when she finally went to the little local market it had closed early, it being Christmas Eve.

Fieldlily, who was always depressed and didn't like celebrations in any case, had received bad news a few days before Christmas regarding his daughter. It was a genuine crisis for him this time. She had been sent to live with an aunt out of state temporarily, pending investigation of her bus driver, who was accused of molesting her. She was 14. Her mother, angry that Fieldlily hadn't paid child support ever since he stopped working, had not seen fit to inform Fieldlily of all this. In fact, when Fieldlily had called at Thanksgiving, she had lied, saying his daughter was "Just visiting" her aunt "for a while." Since it was the end of Thanksgiving vacation, and since the mother of his daughter often used the excuse that Caroline couldn't miss school (she has to do well in school!) to deny Fieldlily visits with her, this sounded off to Charity. Why would she be staying over when she just had a long break from school? Charity thought, not unreasonably.

The next time Fieldlily called, Caroline "wasn't there." When he called again, demanding to speak to his daughter, her mother finally admitted what had happened, and that furthermore, the aunt wanted custody of her, and there was a hearing in two weeks. As to why Fieldlily wasn't told any of this until now, or what was being done to prosecute this molesting bus driver (other than he had lost his job driving the bus - thank God!) or when or if Fieldlily was going to be informed of the custody change, she wouldn't say.

So Fieldlily was in the midst of a real crisis, an ugly one, at that, and Charity felt for him. She called a judge she knew, to run the legality of all this by him and to get his input as to what they should do, but it was Christmas and he wasn't in.

Meanwhile, under the circumstances, she felt a subdued Christmas was the only fitting way to get through the day. Andrew came by to open his presents and left again, to go to his father's for his father's version of a "normal American family Christmas," which was about as real as a blue Dynel Christmas tree. He said he'd be back to spend the night at home because "one night was about all I could take of those people."

Charity, who had cramps most of the day, wouldn't you know it? finally made a hasty version of Chinese chicken and broccoli late in the evening, which she and Fieldlily didn't even eat together, as he was on the phone, consoling Caroline, who really only wanted to come and live with him. She wasn't even hungry, herself. The whole situation - the bus driver, the lying mother, the custody question - had sickened her.

When her sister called, to say thanks for the gifts and merry Christmas, Charity told her what was going on. This lead to a discussion of what had happened when Chloe had been visiting three years ago, and of things from their childhood that had traumatized them, and ended with both of them concluding how much they meant to one another, and a healing of the rift between them, and even a healing, for Charity, of some of that childhood trauma.

"I'll pray for you, and Caroline, too," Chloe said. "Thank you," said Charity.

January 6

Epiphany

The second day back at school after vacation, and it felt like there had never been a break. The bell rang for her third period class. Charity arranged the desks. The kids shuffled in and proceeded to rearrange the desks to satisfy their own sense of order, which seldom coincided with Charity's.

Once they all settled in, more or less, Charity gave the day's assignment - they were reading the play "Twelfth Night" by Shakespeare. They all began clamoring for parts. This always amazed Charity - they didn't usually volunteer to read - but they all had a dramatic streak, and loved emoting by reading their parts.

Sam was unusually quiet. Then he blurted out, "I'm not working. I'm very depressed. Call my social worker! I'm dying. I feel like jumping out the window."

Charity considered this for a moment. Sam often threatened to jump out the window when he was upset by something outside of school. Charity decided to implement a little reality therapy.

"It won't do you a bit of good, Sam, look out those windows."

Sam did, and quickly saw that the roof of the new addition was at window level.

"That's true," he said, and sat down, and asked to be the narrator.

January 11

I want to go home, Charity thought irrationally. It sounded so silly. She was home - in her snug, overstuffed little rented house. "This always was an overstuffed house," her land lady had once remarked, approvingly, when she saw Charity's books crowding the living room shelves. Where else, in Ohio, which she left years ago? Not there, with her father dead, the house sold, and her mother remarried and settled in a retirement condo. So where?

Plus she had always wanted a family, and now she had one, of sorts, the courts having awarded custody of Caroline to her and Fieldlily, and Andrew still at home.

It didn't feel right. It didn't feel like home and family. Fieldlily and also Caroline didn't really like cats, but Charity did. That was one reason she kept them. She also perceived that she and cats shared certain preferences in common. Cats hated having their environment rearranged, or changed in any way. In particular, older, settled cats disliked having newcomers such as kittens or puppies introduced into their homes. This was close to what Charity was feeling; what she was struggling against. With the arrival of Caroline, her home life was in an upheaval, and she didn't like it. The matter of a room for Caroline, for one thing. They

Charity Begins at Home 211

had two bedrooms and one family room and a pull out couch in the living room, which was suitable for visits but not a permanent bedroom. It was too open, for one thing. This meant Charity would feel pressured to give up her precious work space, her therapy room, which was what now occupied the family room. She naturally didn't want to do this. And the phone - Caroline was covered by an order of protection from her molester, who was forbidden to contact her at all - in person or by phone or mail. Fieldlily wanted the number changed to an unlisted one, which Charity *didn't* want. It meant that people who had come for massage in the past and might want to call for appointments again would have no way of reaching her. Of course, she would have nowhere to work if her therapy room was taken. So she felt displaced in her own home.

Caroline also could not go to school, as her molester might try to contact her there, or even abduct her; or Caroline might try to sneak phone calls to him from school. This is what she had done at school in her aunt's town, where she had been before.

So Charity would have to arrange for home teaching. She ventured a proposal to Fieldlily that she might apply to home tutor Caroline and get reimbursed for one or two courses – after all, she had home taught out of school students before for the same district. Fieldlily thought this was an excellent idea. "You could bring in more money for our move," he said enthusiastically, "this could work out well!"

Great, Charity thought, just what she needed. More hours in her already over extended work life. Ugh! Well, she'd need the extra money, because with Caroline added to her health insurance, even more would be deducted from her scant pay at the Academy.

She had to acknowledge that she was feeling resentful of Caroline, and unfairly blaming her for all that had transpired. She just didn't feel warmly toward her just now. She fantasized about Fieldlily leaving, with Caroline, and taking this messy situation out of her life. She had to admit, she didn't feel warmly toward Fieldlily, either, and hadn't for some time. He certainly stinted on affection towards her and Andrew, and also on helping out around the house. Depressed all day, and confessing boredom at night, he let dishes and garbage and dust pile up around him while Charity toiled at two jobs and lacked energy to take on all the disorder when she finally arrived home.

She realized that it was difficult to feel fond of the child if she resented the parent; because she didn't like Fieldlily at this point, it was hard to separate her feelings for Caroline from her feelings for him and to like her, at this point, especially since her arrival in their lives had been sudden, traumatic, and complicated.

No doubt Fieldlily would say this was some neurotic failing on her part. No doubt.

January 13

Mondays in January were always grim. This one was no different and Charity didn't feel like teaching. The kids picked up on this, of course. Monday was vocabulary day, but nobody was looking up words. Terrence picked up Charity's graduate school textbook. "Hey! Can I borrow this?" "No, I need it for school," Charity replied. "Teachers go to school, too?" He responded, amazed.

Meanwhile, Jesse had been carrying around a rolled-up placemat, a nice one, which looked hand woven to Charity. He claimed his brother had made it in prison. "He's in for murder," Jesse announced proudly. "This is his Muslim prayer rug," he said. "What? Let me see that," said Douglass who professed to be a Muslim. He put the absurdly small mat on the floor and contorted himself on it. "It's too small - how d'you get your feet up on it?"

"They can't have 'em big in prison," Jesse explained. "They can't have sheets or nothing either, cuz they hang themselves with 'em where he is."

"Anything. They can't have anything," Charity muttered. This was supposed to be English class after all. "You see?" said Jesse. "She knows."

Later that Day

"Mom, do you know where that copy of Slaughterhouse Five is that you lent me?" Andrew asked Charity, "I'm finished with my last book and I need something to read." Andrew had been reading voraciously during his break. His last book had been stories by H. P. Lovecraft. Charity had written a term paper on the genre of Lovecraft and others in her undergraduate years. She suggested that if he liked Lovecraft, he'd enjoy Ambrose Bierce. "Ok," Andrew agreed, "I really like that whole style of writing. It's like the kind of stories I want to write."

What? Charity thought to herself, beginning to glow inside. Reading constantly, wanting to write, this is my kid, all right!

January 14

What Doesn't Kill Us Makes Us Stronger

That was the thought that kept running through Charity's mind. She wanted to finish her English literature Master of Arts degree. At first it had seemed easy. She went back to the university English department and talked to the graduate chairman. Remembering Charity, he welcomed her and recommended two courses to fulfill the requirements. He called graduate studies. They said reapply.

Reapplication fee would be $50. They also needed two official transcripts at $5 each, and three letters of recommendation. Plus the tuition, with all the fees, came to $1500. So Charity applied for a no-interest loan through the Academy and asked the director, principal, and a board of directors member for references.

She waited two weeks and then heard that the loan fund was out of money. She applied for financial aid. She waited two more weeks, and they had yet to send the forms. Time was running out. She received an unexpected boost when a letter arrived from the state teachers' retirement system, saying she had so much money accrued as of June and was eligible for a loan up to 75% of that amount. She called and asked for forms, and received another letter in reply saying no such person was registered. She called back. She *was* registered. She got an application and filled it out. Time was running out. She called the school. She could register up to the first day of the particular class, but there was a registration on Friday, and she could make arrangements to pay at a later time.

Friday she woke up to an ice storm, the first in years, and no electricity. Going out to the kitchen, she lit the stove and her kerosene lamps. She filled as many gallon plastic jugs with water as she could before the tank ran out. Why did everything, even plumbing, depend on electricity? It didn't where she grew up. The only thing that went out when the electricity did was the lights and the TV or radio, if it only ran on electricity and not batteries. Radio! She had to listen for school closings, and she had no batteries! The car - she could go out to the car and listen to the radio.

She put water on the stove to boil for coffee - she preferred the drip method to her electric perc machine, anyway - and went outdoors.

It was beautiful. Everything, the grass, the trees, the wires, the mailbox, the steps, was coated with ice. The sumac and bittersweet looked pink through the glazing. The sky was a dull pewter and the evergreens were a brilliant gray-green. It all worked together beautifully. Charity appreciated winter for a minute, then went to her car.

Of course the Academy was closed, as were all the schools in four counties. The university had a two hour delayed opening. Good! She hoped they would sand the roads by then, because come hell or ice, she was going to register.

She went back inside her now warm kitchen, and poured coffee. She sat down and all the pets gathered around. They sensed it wasn't an ordinary morning. She let Malcolm up from the cellar, which was his preferred sleeping place, it being cooler and he having at least 20 of his hundred pounds in fur. She felt like she was in a farmhouse kitchen a hundred years ago. It was 6:20 in the morning.

She drank her coffee, ate a bagel, and made plans. She'd have to call the electric company to make them aware of the outage and the reason - a huge branch from the enormous old elm tree had cracked and was lying across the main wires in front of the house.

She'd have to wash using the water she had gathered. She'd have to dress warmly - her Icelandic sweater! She hadn't needed it at all that winter, up to now it had been incredibly warm. She'd have to salt the steps and pathway and find some wood for the stove in her therapy room, because she had a massage client later that day and she didn't intend to lose the money to the weather.

At 10:00 am she was driving down her road, which had been sanded, a minor miracle; someone must have complained. It wasn't her, although she had been tempted to. Andrew was driving this winter, after all. She wanted the roads clear.

She arrived at the university and found the parking lot cleared of ice with plenty of parking spaces, due to the weather. That was the only thing that went smoothly that morning.

She went to the registration area, and they had no record of her, so she was sent to the records office, who said she could register, but the one required course needed approval of the English graduate chair, and the English offices were closed until classes started the following week. With all the complications even getting to this point, Charity should have expected more impediments. Nevertheless, she was exasperated. She didn't trust that just waiting for the first day of classes would clear everything up. She wanted to make sure it all was in place before she left campus that day. So she was sent by the nice young clerk upstairs to the graduate studies office to see the dean. When she got there, the dean had left, but a nice motherly receptionist patiently searched through three filing areas until she found Charity's file. She explained it was waiting for the English department's ok to re-matriculate Charity and then "all systems were go." This woman was truly helpful. She went through Charity's file - which dated from 23 years ago to now - and found a hand- written note from the English department giving her permission to register for any classes she wanted, including the required Shakespeare course. Charity went back to records and showed the nice young clerk her copy of the note from the English department. She explained that Charity would have to get one more ok, from the Recorder, and then she could be officially registered. The Recorder readily signed it, and Charity went back to the clerk, who printed out a schedule and explained that they would bill her.

Charity trudged back to the registration room and showed her schedule to the first woman she spoke to. Everyone had been so nice that day! This woman printed out a bill and sent her to the Bursar to arrange a deferment, as Charity's pension loan hadn't come through yet. She even waived the late fee. After a 45 minute wait, Charity saw the Bursar and he approved her deferment and waiver. He then told her to go and get her student ID, one more thing, and she'd be "all set."

She went to the ID office, and the person in charge was her old neighbor. They caught up on what they were doing and how grown up their children now were and then Charity paid 10 more dollars and she was in.

She didn't remember it being such an ordeal twenty plus years ago, but she was younger and she didn't have to pay for it herself, then. Amazingly, tuition had increased to nearly four times what it had been. Charity wished she had gone back earlier, when it was cheaper and she had tuition waivers from supervising student teachers. Oh, well. Now all she had to do was hope she could handle the work.

January 18

That night, Charity was feeling at loose ends. Fieldlily, whose latest religious venture was the Pentacostal Church, went with Caroline, who he hadn't allowed out of his sight, to a prayer meeting. It was his latest religion of the month, except with Fieldlily it usually lasted longer than a month, his intensity building and building, and then, suddenly, it was over, and all the persons he had convinced that this, finally, was The Way, why didn't they join him and check it out, were left alone, just as suddenly cut adrift, now helpless in Fieldlily's wake as he pursued the next Way. This was proof to Charity that he was still not getting in touch with the divine within himself. The fact that he needed so many outer confirmations backed this up. When you really know, you know and nothing changes it. Besides intense, he was also tense. He was so tense that just getting through his day was an isometric exercise.

So, feeling somewhat bereft and overwhelmed at the prospect of yet another person to provide for, and less money coming in, what with having Caroline on her health insurance, increasing deductions from her pay at the Academy, Charity called her mother. She still didn't know about the abrupt addition of Caroline to her family circle.

Charity Begins at Home 221

When Charity had related all the events of the past ten days, her mother, predictably, was aghast. "What!" She asked, incredulously, "You can't afford another mouth to feed! What is Felipe doing about this? Does he have any income to help you out? This is his responsibility, you know!" Charity explained that, yes, she knew, all too well. Privately, she thought, I wish he'd either start to contribute or leave, preferably the latter. She realized her mother was suggesting the same thing.

"Well, yes, mother, I suppose you're right, but I have trouble putting people who have nothing out on the street." "Well, I wouldn't have trouble with it!" her mother said. What could she say? It was the first time she and her mother agreed whole heartedly.

"Well, let me tell you about your aunty Helene," her mother changed the subject. "Aunty" Helene was an old friend of her mother's. They had worked together when Charity was a child and stayed friends ever since. "Aunty" Helene was English, held two doctorates, and was a formidable role model. When Charity was younger, she had asked her if she might call her by her first name, and she had said, "Certainly, if you call me aunt. I could accept being called Aunty Helene." And so Charity and Chloe had acquired an aunt. She was a wonderful aunt, always giving educational games that made learning painless and fun, the sort of things that you didn't realize were educational until much later in life. She also said, frequently, that one should prepare for the second 40 years of life. She advocated an entirely new profession. She herself had gone on to earn a second doctorate at 40. "Aunty" Helene had just celebrated, Charity's mother informed her, her hundredth birthday, on the very day that Charity and Fieldlily had been given custody of Caroline. She had granted an interview to the newspapers. "There's a picture, but it's awful," her mother said, "but how good can you look at one hundred, for goodness sake!" She went on to add "a good thing her eyesight is so poor now. She'd hate the photo." She had outlived three husbands and survived cancer 25 years before. "I'll send you a clipping," Charity's mother said. "Goodbye, I don't want to run up your bill!"

Charity got off the phone, and reflected on all the strong women in her life, from childhood on up to now. There was "aunty" Helene, 100 and going strong. There was her mother, petite, but strong-willed, and a prevailer against many odds. There was her grandmother, her father's mother, who had refused to stop moving and achieving until her ninetieth birthday, and then decided that winter that she had lived long enough, and was dead in a week of kidney failure. Before she had died, she told Charity a story about her mother, who in one equally tough winter, had looked out and spotted a deer trapped on an ice floe in the Ohio River. She had grabbed a butcher knife, gone outdoors and killed the deer, then gutted it and cut it up. "Times were bad, and meat was scarce, so when she saw the deer, she just did what she had to do to feed her family," her grandmother told Charity.

There was her piano teacher, Mrs. Smith, whom Charity had studied with from the time she was seven until she left for college, Charity keeping in touch with her even then until her death 5 years after that. She was an excellent music teacher, and a hard taskmaster, with strong but well-thought out opinions, and at times Charity felt that she understood her better than her own parents did. Her influence affected Charity right up to the present.

Then there was her seventh grade honors English teacher, who taught diagramming until her students' writing was nearly perfect, and who once admonished Charity, "don't think, know!" when Charity said she thought she'd prepared for an assignment.

So many strong women, right up to now. Her therapist, who showed Charity how to be gentle, generous, productive, and still be strong; even her feisty younger sister. So many strong women in her life. So much influence. This year she was going to be 47.

It was time to join their numbers.

Thanks to Ione, whose support and encouragement led to the creation of this work, to Pauline Oliveros, Lisa Barnard, Matt Goldpaugh, Bill Stevens, and Peter Sorrentino, all of whom had a hand in bringing this final product into being. If I've forgotten anyone else's contribution, please know it is my oversight, and not a slight.

Manufactured By: RR Donnelley
Breinigsville, PA USA
August, 2010